TIME MESSENGER

TIME MESSENGER

BY F. JAY FALONE

Tate Publishing & Enterprises

Published by Tate Publishing & Enterprises, LLC
127 E. Trade Center Terrace | Mustang, Oklahoma 73064 USA
1.888.361.9473 | www.tatepublishing.com

Tate Publishing is committed to excellence in the publishing industry. The company reflects the philosophy established by the founders, based on Psalm 68:11,
"The Lord gave the word and great was the company of those who published it."

Book design copyright © 2008 by Tate Publishing, LLC. All rights reserved.
Cover design by Jonathan Lindsey
Interior design by Nathan Harmony

Published in the United States of America

ISBN: 978-1-60604-862-7
1. Fiction: Science Fiction: Adventure   2. Fiction: Science Fiction: General
08.07.16

1.

It was finally here, the day they had all been waiting for, the test run on the time displacement system. The development of the system had taken ten years and millions of dollars in research and development from their financier Mr. Ross.

Dominick Costa was an MIT graduate with a PhD in physics and had a passion for paleontology. He absently adjusted the brim of his favorite Red Sox cap, mind consumed with the system's details, as he waited in the drive-through line at the coffee shop near his lab. The heat in Framingham was already oppressive at 6 a.m. on an August morning; his baseball jersey, bearing 34 for David Ortiz on the back, as always, felt uncomfortably sweaty.

Consumed equally by his need for a caffeine fix and his

excitement over the system, he almost tapped the bumper of the car in front of him before he reminded himself to pay attention to driving.

The lab was a formerly abandoned battery manufacturing facility for General Motors located just down the street from the former General Motors assembly plant. The brick building itself was very unassuming and looked like many other buildings built in the area around the 1920s and 1930s. Its few windows were above eye level, perfect for keeping out prying eyes; the ceilings were high. There was plenty of room on the roof to install a large climate control system for the supercomputers. They wanted this to be out of sight, not be conspicuous. Part of the attraction to this particular building was that it was located next to a power substation that serviced the assembly plant, so available power would not be an issue; they were planning on consuming a lot of power.

In the beginning phase of converting the building to a lab, a very arrogant public official and a member of the Fire department showed up at the door. The public official was from inspection services and handed Mr. Ross a cease and desist order to immediately stop any further work on the building. Mr. Ross did not obtain any permits or permission to begin the building conversion and the man from inspection services was very clear to point out this fact. Mr. Ross smiled pleasantly and thanked them both. When the two were out of sight, Mr. Ross took out his phone, made a call, and within the hour, the official was back, smiling and apologetic. He had personally delivered the building permit and informed Mr. Ross there would be no further interruption. Again, Mr. Ross smiled and thanked him.

Dominick arrived at the lab at 6:20 a.m. Maria and Mark were already there working; Maria had been there for hours already. Maria D'Luce was also an MIT grad with a PhD in astrophysics. She was tall, thin, had long black hair and was very Italian looking; except for her geekish demeanor with her hair pulled back in a ponytail, MIT sweats and black rimmed glasses, she could have been a model. Dominick adored her. She was the go-to girl, with an IQ of 178. When Maria had something to say about the system, you listened.

Mark Stanton was a Caltech graduate with a PhD in electrical engineering; he was short, wore thick black horn-rimmed glasses, and was much more comfortable communicating with machines than with people. When it came to tech stuff, it seemed there wasn't much he couldn't put together and get working. Especially with the seemingly endless resources provided to them by Mr. Ross. Mark had asked Mr. Ross at one point about the amount of money available and the amount spent, and in a polite way Mr. Ross let him know that he would not go down that road.

"Dom, did you sleep in that shirt again?" asked Maria. Dom knew she was joking, He also knew she was aware he had at least five identical David Ortiz T-shirts.

"Maria, it's a home game today against the Yankees. I always sleep in the same shirt until the Yankee series is over; you know we are only five games up on the Yankees, and this could really hurt if we lost this series."

"You and your precious Red Sox. One World Series win in eighty-six years and you treat each game like it's the last."

Mr. Ross arrived precisely at 7:00 a.m. as he did every

day. He was an older man who looked as if he could be in his fifties, despite his long white hair and beard, and wore

unusually large glasses with semi-transparent maroon frames that covered a good part of his face. He had become an eccentric investment legend in the 1960s; he did not enjoy discussions of money or how he attained his wealth. If money or investments were brought up, he did his best to quickly change the subject.

By all accounts he had to be in his eighties, but had surprising energy and mental clarity, and kept himself fit. He always wore baggy pants, an oversized shirt, and usually some form of hat. The team had a hard time understanding why someone with so much money and influence would spend nearly every day at this dingy lab, but he said this was his passion as well.

Mr. Ross had no family and no other apparent hobbies other than working on the time displacement equipment. He had recently given up investing in the stock market to work full-time on the project. He was always smiling and confident, no matter what the setback was; he always reiterated his confidence in the team and how he knew they would get the system up and running.

Mr. Ross was a bit of an enigma: he was clearly willing to give Dom or the others the shirt off his back, but would not get into his personal life much, just mentioning that he was adopted, grew up in the Midwest, and never knew his real parents.

He was also the scientific catalyst for the project. He had research and notes on advanced physics that did not appear in any textbook. At first this was cause for concern for Dom,

Maria, and Mark; they all wondered how such physics had not been published. Mr. Ross explained to them that he had hired physicists over the last two decades to expand on Einstein's theories, and that the work had to remain confidential. It was all above board, and legal. He simply did not want the time travel equations to fall into the wrong hands.

The research had taken years, and he had the equations boiled down to a few pages, which needed to be programmed into the system. He also had the pod design, which he had ordered parts for and he, Mark and Dom assembled. The parts came from at least 30 different vendors, so none of them could have the slightest idea of what the end result would be. If any of them got too curious or asked too many questions, they were replaced in short order. Few of them did; the parts themselves seemed harmless enough, and Mr. Ross was always willing to pay well in excess of the quoted price to get the parts when he needed them.

All of the team had an interest in the asteroid strike sixty-five million years ago that wiped out the dinosaurs. Dom was interested more in the dinosaurs, and Maria was interested in the actual asteroid strike itself. It was thought that an asteroid or comet approximately ten kilometers or six miles wide struck what is now Mexico's Yucatan Peninsula and created a crater 180 km (100 miles) wide and wiped out the dinosaurs and most of all other plants and animals.

The idea was to send back a recording device near the time of the impact, possibly observe some live dinosaurs, and witness the asteroid strike. They could send back as many as they wanted until they recovered one that worked. All they would have to do is send it and it should appear right at the

GPS coordinates they sent it to. If not, they could just keep sending others to different locations until they found one that they could retrieve data from.

"I hope we are able to record some live dinosaurs walking in front of the lens," Dom stated.

"That would be a wonderful bonus, but the odds are against us getting that lucky, we have our work cut out for us just recording the asteroid strike," Maria replied.

"We may need to send back quite a few probes, because after the impact it was thought that a cloud of searing hot gas set most of what was now North America on fire. This probe would not only have to survive sixty-five million years of weather, but the searing heat created by the asteroid strike, while most likely being buried. The badlands of North Dakota seem to be a good spot where dinosaur bones still to this day lie on the ground out in the open," Dom informed Maria.

"Those probes are very tough, Mr. Ross and I took two of them to Marlboro Airport and dropped them out of a chopper at three hundred feet up, didn't even phase them. The probes should survive just about anything but a direct strike. I hope we are that lucky Dom, I would love to see live dinos myself," Mark commented excitedly to Dom and Maria.

"The implications are staggering; we could witness first-hand what, for over hundreds of years, had only been theory," Dom stated.

"If this works, we may be able to send back other probes to observe other historical events," Mark stated.

Mark wanted to send one back to the grassy knoll to see who really shot JFK.

Mr. Ross said, "That would be a good one to let go; let's focus on the sixty-five-million-year-old mystery first." The team was so excited about this they could hardly contain themselves. Mr. Ross, however, just smiled his usual confident smile.

The time displacement equipment could only go back in time (or so it was thought), based on all their calculations. It wouldn't work going forward to what hasn't been yet, only to what has been.

The time displacement equipment was designed to fold time back on itself. This was based on time distortion observed around large planets and stars. The time displacement equipment would enhance this effect in theory to such a degree that traveling to the past would be possible without the mass of a planet or star.

The time displacement equipment basically employed these principles; it was just a question of how much power you put into the system. The more power, the farther back you could go.

"Is the probe ready?" Dom asked. Mark had run the diagnostics on the probe every day for the last four months.

"It is A-1, should last sixty-five million years or so," said Mark.

"I hope you are correct," said Maria. Mr. Ross just smiled as usual. Today's test would not send anything back sixty-five million years, just a minute in time, kind of like Doc Brown's first test on the De Lorean, to see how it worked. They only had to go back one minute, so in theory, before they sent it, one should appear a minute before and for one minute there should be two probes. It took a while for the team to wrap their minds around the temporal mechanics, but the consensus was that there should be two objects present for the amount of time the first object was sent back.

2.

The time displacement equipment itself was an incredible sight. It was about the size of a van or pick-up truck, and nearly every square inch of the exterior was covered with conduits, cooling tubes and wiring. The inside, however, consisted of seemingly seamless black oval walls with no corners, like being inside a flat black egg.

When the door closed, you could barely see any seam; it was pitch-black. There was no lighting; to see inside the team members had to bring in a light source. It was linked to two Cray supercomputers, for which Mark had written every line of code and run and re-run diagnostics hundreds of times. The control panel had a large monitor and sliding potentiometers to control power; Mark had designed them to look like the transporter control in the original *Star Trek* series, of which he was a huge fan.

Mark would soon be at the controls of this history making device, he could hardly control his enthusiasm.

The hope was, when they turned on the system, they would not draw power at levels that would draw the attention of the local authorities. Mark said he could ramp up the power gradually to the needed level, but there was no guarantee.

"Ready to go where no man has gone before?" said Mark.

Maria replied, "Ready to go where *no one* has gone before; I am a Next Gen fan." She enjoyed the playful *Star Trek* quips as much as Mark did.

The first test would be to just turn the system on and bring it fully operational, something that had not been tried yet.

Mark sat at his station and started typing; the system came on line and the power-up test was ready to begin.

Maria said, "Engage," with a big smile.

Mark replied, "Aye Aye, captain."

Mark ever so slightly pushed up on the slide controls and a low-frequency pulsating hum began to emit from the pod; it was eerie how the pulsating sound seemed to penetrate right through them, yet it was on the lowest power setting.

"Take us to Warp One," said Maria.

Mark had 10 increments on the slide control, which he had labeled Warp 1 through Warp 10. The familiar "Aye Aye, captain" was his reply. As he pushed up the slide control, the pulsating frequency increased and you could see the pod begin to glow a deep red through the observation window in the pod room. The red glow was pulsating in sync with the now much louder low-frequency sound and more pronounced vibration.

Dom was concerned that the sound and vibration would attract attention outside the building so he ran outside to see if any sound or vibration could be noticed; it was amazing, but there was absolutely no indication outside that the system was running.

The sound and vibration seemed trapped within a localized area within the pod room.

Mark began to slide the controls up. The pulsating became more of an even hum; the pod was glowing deeper red and small items in the pod room began to be pulled toward the pod. It was creating a gravity well, an artificial black hole in the Pod room!

"Power down," said Maria. Mark slowly pulled the slide back to zero.

"That was impressive, but now let's give it a real test," said Mr. Ross.

Mark picked up a coffee cup and went over to the pod. He opened the door; it was warm, and he placed the cup inside on the floor. "Let's try sending it back ten minutes, so when we open the door to put the cup in, it should already be there if the test is to be successful." The cup wasn't there when the door was opened.

Mr. Ross smiled, "There has to be a first time for a time loop to begin, and if this is the first time, the cup wouldn't be there yet, don't you agree?"

They all nodded in agreement. Mark entered the destination coordinates in the system, clearing the negative sixty five million years entry he had programmed in previously.

Mark slowly powered up the system to one, then three, then five, then slowly up to ten.

"Ready?" said Mark.

"Do it," replied Mr. Ross.

Mark hit the commit button. There was a flash of white light, and the system began to power down on its own as it was programmed to do. Dom went to the door and opened it, there was nothing inside.

Maria, Mark, and, Dom had blank looks on their faces. Mr. Ross had his usual confident smile.

"It looks like we failed. Back to the drawing board," said Dom.

Maria, scratching her head, said, "It had to go somewhere."

"Yes, but where? Perhaps it didn't go anywhere. Maybe we somehow broke down the electric bonding that holds matter together, and we simply disintegrated it?" said Mark.

"Possibly you watched the original *War of the Worlds* one time too many. You are pretty much quoting Gene Barry after the first Martian attack," teased Dom.

Mr. Ross had an idea. "Humor me on this, folks. Mark could you please program in exactly one year back to the second?"

Mark replied, "I can, if you give me a few minutes to modify the code. I did not program in a provision for seconds, it didn't seem necessary where we were going to send the probes back millions of years, but it is easily done."

Mark began typing. Maria, Dom, and Mr. Ross inspected the pod while Mark was programming. It was warm, but cooling quickly; it was surprising how quickly it cooled.

Maria suggested, "I don't think it was really the pod getting hot. I think it was more we simulated a black hole that was radiating energy."

Dom and Mr. Ross looked at each other and Dom replied, "Of course," playfully.

About ten minutes later, Mark said, "We are ready to go."

"Dom will you open the pod please? I am going to put in a test subject that is appropriate for the occasion." Mr. Ross pulled out a toy dinosaur from his pocket, similar to the models Dom had on his desk. He wrote the date on the bottom of the dinosaur in black Sharpie pen, 08/24/07, showed it to the team, placed it in the pod, and closed the door.

Mark began the power-up sequence to full power and everyone held on. Minus sixty five million years came up; he cleared it once again and entered minus one year exactly to the second. He hit the commit button. There was again a flash of white light, and the pod powered down.

Dom opened the door, it was empty. "What are we doing to this stuff? Are we disintegrating it?"

"I don't believe so," said Mr. Ross. "Dom, those dinosaurs on your desk, where did you get those?"

"You know, I am not sure I remember where they all came from. I have been collecting them over the years."

"Just one in particular, that Brachiosaurus, where did you get that?"

Dom pondered for a moment. "I found that one on the floor of the pod room before we moved the pod there." They all looked at each other.

Dom ran to his desk, picked up the dinosaur, and turned it over. 08/24/07 was written on it in black Sharpie.

3.

Mr. Ross wore his characteristic smile. "I believe we need one more test. Maria, what do you think happened?"

She smiled and said, "I believe I know where you are going with this. You sent the dino back exactly one year to the second because we did not account for the Earth's orbit or rotation, correct?"

"Exactly."

Mark and Dom were not astrophysicists and looked slightly dumbfounded. "Maria, what are you talking about?" asked Dom.

"I think we all are victims of watching too much science fiction time travel. If we send something back exactly one minute in time, that exact point, which is approximately on the surface of the Earth one minute ago, will no longer be the same location. The Earth is orbiting the sun at approximately thirty kilometers per second, so the coffee cup we sent back ten minutes will be eighteen thousand kilometers in back of Earth's orbit around the Sun.

In other words, simply, the Earth has moved from where it was ten minutes ago. The cup is floating in space where the Earth was ten minutes ago. In about one years time the Earth, due to its orbit around the sun, will come back to this approximate point in its orbit and run into the cup. This will cause the cup to burn up in the Earths atmosphere.

Maria paused. "We also will have to account for the Earth's rotation if we are to get an exact fix on where the object will appear. So, when we sent back the dinosaur exactly one year to the second, the dinosaur appeared in the exact same spot one year ago. Dom found it on the floor and just added it to his collection; none of us realized that we had witnessed a successful test of our system one year ago."

"Wow," was all Mark could muster.

With that Maria squeezed Doms' hand and whispered, "We did it."

Dom chimed in, "Holy crap, we just invented the cheapest way to launch payloads into orbit in the history of space travel. If Doc Brown's DeLorean had worked, it would have been the first car in space. Poor Einstein (Doc Brown's dog) would not have made it."

Mr. Ross said, "Correct, but let's not jump the gun. We should do one more test, a test that will put something into orbit we can track." All agreed.

"We could send back one of the dino probes," Mark said. "They were designed to last sixty-five million years; it has a locator beacon and a camera, so we can photograph the stars compared to recent star charts and determine its time of arrival based on star locations. The probes were not designed to transmit digital photos, but I can add this feature without too much trouble, since there is already a fairly powerful transmitter on board."

Mark began to dissect one of the probes and Dom and Maria began their calculations.

Maria explained to Dom, "Looking down on our solar system, the Earth and all other planets orbit the sun in a clockwise motion. Also, Earth spins in a clockwise motion on a twenty-four hour cycle. So, sending something back in exactly one-year increments would be the easiest way to have it land back on Earth, otherwise there would be a re-entry system required."

Dom sat at the table next to Maria, and they both began their calculations.

Maria began mumbling equations to herself. "Vt $=2.978589 \times 10$ to the 4th meters per second, equatorial diameter = 12,756 kilometers..." Dom had his calculator out and was scratching notes down on an old yellow legal pad. They worked on their calculations for several minutes.

Maria spoke, first looking at Dom, then to the others. "If we send something back one year minus one hour, that's 3600 seconds away. That's about 108,000 km in front of the Earth's orbital path. At thirty kilometers per second and accounting for the diameter of the Earth, we will have one hour of tracking time, provided we send the probe when

Earth is facing the correct direction. In other words, the launch should occur when the Earth's rotation is facing the leading edge of its orbit, and not when it is on the trailing edge or the back side of the rotation. The only down side is that the probe will be out there nearly a year waiting for the Earth to catch up with it. All we have to worry about are micrometeors and other things that may bump into it."

"I agree, Maria, but these probes are designed to take quite a beating. Although they haven't been tested for the cold of space, they should be okay. If they are not, we have time on our side. We can just keep sending them back until we get a probe that works, the same way we were going to send them back to observe the sixty-five-million-year-old meteor strike, but now they only have to last one year. Piece of cake," said Mark.

Dom spoke up, "I got the same numbers. I calculate we can launch in fourteen hours and fifty-three minutes." All were in agreement.

"Anyone hungry?" Mr. Ross asked.

"I am, let's go grab something to eat at La Cantina," Maria said.

Mark said, "I have got a few hours to go on the probe. Can you send something back?"

"No problem. You want the same as usual?" asked Dom.

"Of course." Mark loved the gnocchi and meatballs from La Cantina, an Italian restaurant over on Route 135, to the point that if left to his own devices that was probably all he would ever eat. The restaurant was a favorite of all of them; the good food and close location made them regulars, and they were on a first-name basis with just about everyone who worked there.

Maria and Dom sat next to each other, across the table from Mr. Ross.

While eating, Mr. Ross asked, "What do you think of these implications? Would either of you ever want to become time travelers yourselves?"

Dom answered first, "Are you kidding? I would be scared stiff, but no way I could pass up a chance of a lifetime like that. But I think constructing a pod large enough to carry a re-entry vehicle may be a ways off. And the amount of power required would be staggering. The folks that run the power grid wouldn't be too happy if we sucked them dry. I am not even sure, without calculations, that the grid could handle it. I don't know how much money you have, but that could be a bank breaker."

"It's just a hypothetical question, Dom, but I see this is something you would do if the opportunity presented itself," said Mr. Ross. "Maria, how about you?"

"Mr. Ross, to be honest, I would be shaking in my boots. But if the opportunity presented itself and it seemed relatively safe, I can't see how I could turn down an opportunity like that. What the heck, I would go for it. Someone has to hold Dom's hand so he wouldn't chicken out." Dom blushed a bit and had trouble containing his smile.

"Well, I guess that settles it. If we ever do get to that point, you two will have to be the world's first time travelers," said Mr. Ross. Dom and Maria both laughed.

"Sure Mr. Ross, sign us on. We are ready to go," said Dom.

"Tomorrow's a big test and a big day. I am going to drop

off Mark's food on the way home to Dover, since it's right on the way. Why don't you two head home and get some rest? We can all meet at the lab early tomorrow. This has been a big day already and we could all use some sleep," said Mr. Ross.

"Sounds good. See you in the morning. Good night, Mr. Ross, and good night, Dom." Maria squeezed Dom's hand under the table, and this time he couldn't control his smile.

"See you all in the morning. Good night Maria," whispered Dom, as he floated out on cloud nine.

They all walked to their cars. Mr. Ross got into his usual Cadillac. He collected them and had them stored in his climate-controlled garage at his home in Dover.

After Maria and Dom drove off, he pulled a phone from the console with only two buttons on it: "Send" and "End."

He pushed the green Send button, someone answered immediately. "Get the team ready."

"Understood" was the response, and Mr. Ross pressed the End button.

4.

Mr. Ross arrived at the lab at 5:30 a.m., breaking his usual routine of 7:00 a.m. for this special occasion.

Mark had slept at the lab on a cot in his office, his takeout container on the floor beside him. He did this quite often, and Mr. Ross often brought him dinner at the lab. Mr. Ross felt for Mark and his lack of social skills. Mark respected Mr. Ross' opinion and based on their conversations he was joining clubs and social groups to learn how to interact better. Mr. Ross' advice was starting to pay dividends, over the past few months. Mark was actually starting conversations and going out with friends other than Maria and Dom.

Maria and Dom arrived together, not long after Mr. Ross. Both had had trouble sleeping last night with such a big day in store. Dom kicked Mark's cot. Mark groaned and sat up. Without a word he reached up and Dom put an extra large coffee with extra cream and extra sugar in his hand. Mark took a few big gulps and staggered to his feet. "Feeling okay?" asked Dom.

Mark grunted what appeared to be yes.

"Don't step in the takeout container," Dom warned.

"Okay thanks," said Mark.

"Doesn't that hurt when you chug hot coffee?" Dom asked.

Mark replied in geek fashion, "Pain receptors are not online yet. I will get back to you in a few minutes." Dom laughed.

Mark continued, "I was up later than I expected. You know those small solar panels that got delivered by mistake a few months ago? Well I connected them to the probe and added a small heating element and some insulation. Where the probe is a sealed unit, a little heat and insulation will give us some insurance of success. Good thing we didn't return those panels. They seemed to be the exact size we needed. If I was going to order panels, these are what I would have ordered; the assortment of heaters we had in stock seems weird also. It seemed as if whatever I needed just happened to be here, so I wished for a hot blonde. That didn't work, so I just put the probe together."

"Nice work, Mark. Just in case for next time, try a suitcase full of hundred-dollar-bills," Dom joked.

"Will do," said Mark.

"Excellent thinking Mark, shall we load the probe into the pod?" asked Mr. Ross. The probe itself wasn't too heavy, only about one hundred pounds, but with the solar panels it was awkward to handle. Mark and Dom loaded it on a flat cart and slowly rolled it into the pod.

Mark went over to the control panel and began to enter the destination. "So we are attempting to send back the probe exactly minus 8765 hours?"

"Correct, 365.25 days times, twenty-four hours a day equals 8,766 hours in a year and we are sending the probe back one year minus one hour. The Earth should overtake the probe quickly, so do we have the receiver tuned and working?" asked Maria.

"Yes, I tested it last night and I was getting some inter-ference. Someone was using the same frequency, but it was fairly weak and it should not interfere with our test today," Mark replied.

Mr. Ross was listening to them and said with his usual confidence and smile, "Okay, let's power up."

Just as Mark began to power up, everything went dark. The emergency lighting came on quickly, and the back-up genera-tor turned on. The generator could run the basic systems, but did not have enough power to run the test. "Is that a blackout, I hope, and not a system overload?" Maria asked.

"I will go outside and see if any of the other buildings have power," Mr. Ross said. As he walked outside, he saw a power company van there. The power company worker had obviously cut the power to the building and had a police detail with him.

The power company official in a suit accompanied by two lineman strode up to Mr. Ross, very agitated. "We traced yesterday's power consumption to this substation and to you. Do you know how much power you pulled through these lines?" He was practically yelling. Two police officers stood directly behind him with stern looks on their faces. "You caused a brown-out to this area yesterday. Do you know how many complaints and calls we had?"

One of the police officers said, "Could I see your identification please?" Mr. Ross complied with his usual calm and smile.

"I believe I can clear this all up if you will allow me to make one quick call?"

The officer replied, "Sir, the power company is here to shut down the power, if you cause any problems, we will be forced to take you in. But if you make a call that could shed some light on this, feel free."

Mr. Ross smiled and pulled his phone out of his pocket. He pressed the green button. "Sir, I am here at the lab with two Framingham police officers and some gentlemen from the power company. They have turned off the power and plan to leave."

The reply was "Understood, stand by."

"If you gentlemen can wait about one minute, this will all be cleared up," he said politely to the others.

"We can't do that, Mr. Ross. If you would please come inside with us, we need a few questions answered. Other officers are on the way to padlock the lab until this all gets sorted out."

Mr. Ross smiled and said, "Of course Officer, if that is how you have to proceed."

As the officer gestured toward the door, he got a call on his police radio from his captain. "Officer Reynolds."

"Yes, sir."

"Release Mr. Ross at once and return to the station, priority one."

"Yes, sir," the officer replied with a confused expression on his face. Knowing the captain as well as he did, the tone in his voice suggested he not ask any questions.

The power company official couldn't believe what was happening. "Are you two just leaving? You have got to be kidding! You can't leave, where are you going?" he yelled at the police officers in a near frenzy. At that moment his personal cell phone rang. He looked at the phone and saw that it was the main office number. Although still a bit in a frenzy, he answered the phone. It was the president of the power company."

"Tim? May I call you Tim?"

"Yes sir."

"Please restore power to the building and make sure they have all the power they need, do what you can to make sure there will be no further interruptions, then report to my office."

"Ahhh, yes, sir," Tim replied, first with an expression of disbelief, and then as he thought about it a bit, the expression turned to worry about reporting to the president.

Mr. Ross smiled, thanked everyone, and walked back into the building. The power came back on immediately.

Mark said, "We need a few minutes to re-boot. What happened?"

"A minor interruption. It won't happen again. Let's get ready to test."

Mark began the power-up sequence to full power and everyone held on. The minus sixty-five million years came up; he cleared it once again and entered minus 8,765 hours to the second. He hit the commit button, there was again a flash of white light, and Mark powered down. Dom opened the door and it was empty.

"Is anything being transmitted?" asked Maria.

"Yes! We have a strong signal! Calculated distance from source, 100,000 kilometers. We did it! Downloading star charts, this should only take a few minutes. This is awesome, I can't wait to review the photos. Hopefully we will catch some UFO's out there sailing around, and get to see some aliens. Download complete, distance from source 90,000 kilometers. That interference stopped as soon as we sent the probe back, but it had the exact same frequency as our probe. I hope it didn't mess up our data."

Mr. Ross smiled as usual and said, "Mark, what you saw as interference at the same frequency was a successful test of our probe that we had not launched yet. Remember we sent it back a year, so it has been out there all this time and we were coming up on it as we were getting to launch. I knew as soon as you said that about the interference, we would be successful."

"Wow, that's cool. We were successful before we even did it."

"Correct," said Mr. Ross with a chuckle, "it is cool. Will you all excuse me for a moment? "

Mr. Ross stepped outside and picked up his phone, then hit the green button. "Now."

"Understood," was the usual response.

Mr. Ross came back in the building and said, "We have all worked very hard, and we could all use a break. I would like all of you to be my guests on a vacation for a short time, so please go home and pack some clothes and meet me here tomorrow morning at 9:00 a.m. sharp. I will not take no for an answer."

The three scientists looked at each other, and then nodded in agreement. "Where will we go?" asked Maria.

Mr. Ross replied, "The most fantastic adventure you could possibly imagine, that's all I am going to tell you. We will be gone a few weeks, so call your family and friends and pack accordingly. This is a trip none of you will ever forget."

Dom said jokingly, "That's quite a build-up. Can you come through on that?"

"I guarantee it, so don't be late," Mr. Ross answered as he left the building.

5

Dominick, Maria, and Mark all arrived at the lab at 9:00 a.m. with their bags in tow. Mr. Ross was waiting outside. "Let's go inside," he said, "and I will prepare you for the trip."

Mark whispered to Dom, "Prepare us for the trip? What the heck is that supposed to mean?"

They all walked in and the three scientists stopped short in awe. Everything inside was gone. The floors looked like they had been polished and the walls were freshly painted, computers, pod, desks, everything... gone!

Maria started, "Mr. Ross, what—"

At that moment the door swung open. Eight men in black uniforms and mirrored sunglasses poured in.

Mr. Ross gesturing to a tall, expressionless man calmly

said, "Maria, Dom, Mark, this is Colonel Jenks." Colonel Jenks was in excellent physical condition. He looked to be in his forties, what could be seen of his hair was salt and pepper in color, mostly dark black.

All three were still in shock. Dom started to say something but the rigid-looking colonel cut him off. "Mr. Costa, Miss D'Luce, and Mr. Stanton, please follow me." The other seven members of the team moved in behind them; given they were armed and had on body armor, it wasn't exactly a request.

Mr. Ross just stood there smiling. "I promised you a trip you wouldn't forget, didn't I?"

Maria managed a nervous smile and Mr. Ross said "Don't worry, trust me please."

Maria shakily answered "Okay," and they shuffled out the door following Jenks. Four black SUVs with black-tinted windows stood, doors open and engines running. The lead SUV had a flashing blue light on its dash, the only SUV without a tinted windshield to allow vehicles in front to see the flashing light and pull out of their way.

"Sergeant," Colonel Jenks ordered, "Please collect all phones and personal communication devices and remove all batteries."

"Yes, sir." After the phones were collected, Maria and Dom were put into one SUV, Mr. Ross and Mark were put into another. The men gathered their bags and were put into another.

One SUV led the convoy, the passengers were in the middle two, and another SUV brought up the rear. Colonel Jenks rode in the front passenger seat of Dom and Maria's SUV. Dom looked at the door; there were no handles, and the glass was tinted so heavily that he could barely see out.

Colonel Jenks looked back expressionlessly and said, "Comfortable?"

Dom and Maria just nodded yes; they were too nervous to complain. After a moment, Dom tried to start up a conversation. When he spoke there was a bit of shaking in his voice and he tried not to sound too nervous. "We seem to be riding a bit heavy, or is it my imagination?"

"Bulletproof," was Jenks' one word answer.

Dom and Maria looked at each other.

Dom tried again. "Are we under arrest or prisoners or something?"

Jenks said nothing and just turned to face the front of the SUV.

Despite the heavy tinting, Dom could see they were headed east on Route 135 into Natick, well in excess of the speed limit. Cars pulled over and let them by. Then they turned on Speen Street and were soon on the Mass Pike East going toward Boston.

Dom tried an attempt at humor to lighten the mood and said, "It's amazing how quickly you can get around with a flashing blue light on the dash."

Jenks ignored him.

At the speed they were traveling, they arrived at Logan International Airport within twenty-five minutes and drove directly onto the tarmac to pull up beside a private jet. The jet had no markings of any kind, was painted flat black, and had an odd shape. The shape was somewhere between a Stealth fighter and Sr-71 Blackbird, but large enough to accommodate passengers.

They all got out of the SUVs at the same time. Dom asked Mr. Ross, "Mr. Ross, yours?" pointing to the jet.

Mr. Ross nodded.

"Why the strange shape?"

"Stealth technology, very difficult to track us once we are in flight," Mr. Ross replied.

Dom started to scratch his head and mumbled "Difficult to track us?"

Jenks spoke up. "Please board." Although he said "Please," the three scientists got the idea "No, thank you" was not an option.

They all climbed the folded-down stairs into the jet. It was surprisingly plush inside: fourteen large reclining leather seats, a fully stocked bar, and refreshments. The cockpit door was open and between the pilot and co-pilot the displays looked like something out of the future, far more advanced that any systems they had ever seen on a plane.

"Please help yourself to the refreshments, we will be taking off in approximately ten minutes," said Mr. Ross.

Mark muttered to himself, "Taking off from Logan within ten minutes of arrival? This was worth the trip just to see that." Mark had traveled to the West Coast and back several times, and consequently had spent hours at Logan due to the tighter security implemented after 9/11.

The door closed and the jet taxied to the runway. "X1, you are cleared for takeoff," was heard from the cockpit.

Maria looked out the window, there were at least ten commercial jets waiting in line to take off. "Don't we have to wait for them to take off first?"

"No," was Jenks' reply. He sat back in his recliner and

began reading his newspaper as the engines powered up and the jet took off.

The jet had surprising power. They all had flown before, but they sensed they were traveling much faster than a private jet should be able to. The pilot announced, "We will be arriving in Nevada at 9:30 a.m. local time."

Maria started running the numbers through her head and said to Mr. Ross, "How can that be? We left Logan just before 10:00 a.m. Even if we are going to Nevada, we should arrive about 1:00 p.m. local time. It's a six-hour flight traveling about 3,000 miles at 500 mph, minus three hours for the time difference. Are we really going to Nevada?"

Mr. Ross replied, "You're quick, of course, Maria. We are going to Nevada, but we are traveling at Mach 1.5 or about 1,140 mph so it's only a 2.6 hour flight. We left about 10:00 a.m., minus three hours for the time difference. Add about two and a half hours' flight time, which comes out to about 9:30 a.m., plus or minus."

"Isn't traveling faster than the speed of sound prohibited over the continental United States?" asked Dom.

"It is allowed under certain circumstances. This happens to be one of them." He paused. "We have a busy day today, so why don't you all get something to eat and try to relax? The bagels are from Einstein Brothers and they are my personal favorite. Dom, there is plenty of coffee, and Mark, if you open the fridge door, there is something special in there for you."

Dom, Maria, and Mark sat close together and at first said nothing. Maria spoke first in a low voice so that none of their "hosts" could hear them.

"If they were going to hurt us, they certainly wouldn't

have taken us in a state of the art private jet to Nevada, and serve us breakfast. We would probably be floating in the Charles River out to Boston Harbor."

Mark nodded in agreement, and said "Obviously there is some bigger picture to the Time Displacement Equipment that has been going on and I think we are going to find out."

Dom nodded in agreement and after taking the time to digest the situation said, "If this is the end, I am going to at least have a coffee."

Mark was next. He got up and looked in the fridge and was in his glory when he saw gnocchi and meatballs. Maria decided to try one of Mr. Ross' favorite bagels.

All three sat together in a close group exchanging nervous glances, looking up at the perpetually smiling Mr. Ross and the emotionless Colonel Jenks for some sign or indication to help them understand the situation.

After they had their breakfast, the three began to sense they were in no immediate danger and tensions eased a bit, although they had essentially been kidnapped by armed men and their major benefactor. The time seemed to pass very quickly.

The pilot announced, "Please return to your seats and fasten your seat belts, we are on our final approach."

It was raining in the distance and Dom admired the lightning show as bolts of lightning flashed within the clouds. "Maria, look at this!"

Maria looked out the window, a little concerned. "Are we far away enough from that lightning to be safe?"

Mr. Ross replied, "We are very safe, please don't worry."

Mark looked out the window. Loving science fiction and science fact as much as he did, he recognized where they were approaching and couldn't help himself. "Dom, Maria look out the window, that's Route 375 and that's Groom Road. We are landing in Area 51!"

Dom and Maria just stared at each other, not daring to speak. They managed to look at Mr. Ross as if to ask why.

He wore his usual smile, and said "Ready for the adventure of a lifetime?"

All they could manage was a nervous smile in return.

The flight was shorter than anticipated, they arrived just after 9:00 a.m. local time. Mark had to comment, "That was a heck of a tail wind or we were going just a tad faster than Mach 1.5."

Colonel Jenks looked up at him with an annoyed expression. The plane touched down effortlessly and smoothly. Colonel Jenks announced, "Everyone please deplane," and they all headed to the exit. "Mr. Stanton, Mr. Costa, and Miss D'Luce, please follow the Airman to the briefing room. We will take care of your bags."

Outside, the storm was just reaching the complex. Mr. Ross pulled the sergeant aside. "Sergeant, please load Miss D'Luce's and Mr. Costa's bags into RV1 along with my bag."

"Are you going as well, sir?" asked the sergeant. He then said, "Sorry, sir." He knew better than to expect a response.

Mr. Ross just smiled. "Also, could you please bring Mr. Stanton's bags into his quarters?"

"Yes, sir."

One of the eight-man team was carrying a locked metal attaché case and moved to Mr. Ross' side as they entered.

General Nichols, an intimidating figure at six foot three, in excellent physical condition in his mid fifties, with graying hair, was in command of the project. He had been there all night installing the control system flown in from Framingham. General Nichols walked briskly to meet Mr. Ross just outside the Hangar door.

"Good morning, General," said Mr. Ross.

"Good morning," replied the general somewhat suspiciously. General Nichols didn't entirely trust Mr. Ross. He didn't understand his motives or interest in the project, and it gave him some pause.

"General, I need the data stored in the case this gentleman is carrying," Mr. Ross said, pointing to the team member with the metal case, "loaded into the RV1 computer right now."

"Just a minute, Mr. Ross. We will have to check the data first to ensure it will not corrupt any of the programming, and I would like to know just what you are putting into my bird."

Mr. Ross smiled, took out his phone and pushed the green button, then turned away so the men couldn't hear what he was saying. He turned back to see the general answering his own identical green-buttoned phone.

"General," sounded through the speaker, "Mr. Ross is now in command of the project. His orders are to be carried out without question and exactly as he describes."

"Sir, I don't recommend—"

"*Now*, General."

"Yes, sir, Mr. President." The general stiffened and glared at Mr. Ross. General Nichols was much more comfortable issuing orders than taking them. Although his response was yes sir, his body language was anything but compliant. It was amazing just how intimidating yes sir could be.

Mr. Ross smiled at the general and said, "I am not in

competition with you, we are on the same team General, there are things that need to be done quickly and at the moment there is not sufficient time to explain. I promise in short order, you will be completely informed as to the situation and you will understand."

With that, the General softened a bit, but still had a suspicious look on his face.

Mr. Ross spoke to the team member carrying the case, "Young man, please deliver the case to the control room to upload the data. Also please stay in the control room until all the data is loaded and report back to me when it is complete."

The team member looked up at the General as if asking permission, the General nodded in an affirmative fashion in his direction.

"Yes sir," was the only response and he was off.

6.

The jet had landed outside a large hangar. Behind the hangar were two large generator systems, so large it looked as if each one could run a good-sized city. They only needed one, but the back-up system was there just in case. They were fueled by natural gas. A long pipeline extended eastward, and tied into the national supply lines, so they would not have to worry about a shortage of fuel. Mr. Ross went inside the hangar where several technicians were finishing up the control system install.

A large door sectioned off the back end of the hangar, which was sliding open as he walked in. Inside the door was a pod. But not just a pod, it was large enough to drive a tractor trailer truck into. All it needed to be operational was the control system Mark had designed. As Mr. Ross entered, an Airman was escorting Mark into the control room.

"Well Mark, what do you think of our little science project?" asked Mr. Ross.

Mark was speechless for a moment, struck in awe by the sheer size of the pod. Then he said, "Cool."

Mr. Ross chuckled. "Yes, it is, Mark."

"Mr. Ross, can you explain—"

"Mark, I know you are curious, and I promise all your questions will be answered in time. But for now, I will ask you to please hold your questions. I will tell you something that might help you to wrap that curious mind of yours around all this. This has obviously been planned for some time and we know the stakes involved. This may sound a bit clichéd, however what you, I, and the team are doing is arguably the most important thing in the history of mankind, and if we fail everyone—every man, woman, and child on the face of the Earth, yourself included—could be gone in a flash. I am not exaggerating when I say this. What we are doing here is of supreme importance; we must not fail. So if you are ready to go where no one has gone before, let's power up the system and run some diagnostics"

Mark looked at Mr. Ross, mouth hanging slightly open, shoulders drooped as if in submission of a greater will. "Uh sure, okay," Mark replied.

"Excellent. Mark, you may have noticed, based on our test in Framingham on the prototype, that we had a small gravity problem. Therefore, no items can be in the room with the pod. We also set it back a safe distance from the controls, with a twelve-inch-thick bulletproof glass wall between the pod and us. We don't know how powerful the gravity well will be. We didn't have time to work that out after we discovered the gravity effect from our Framingham test and when we reach full power we don't want to get sucked into a black hole, now do we?"

Mark didn't answer, but just looked up nervously from the controls.

"Don't worry, Mark," Mr. Ross assured.

Mark began his diagnostics. Each system came up *ready* and after pages of *ready* scrolled down the screen, the *system online* message appeared on the screen. Mark tapped the Enter key and the familiar minus sixty-five million years appeared. "Should I enter a destination time?"

"Not yet," Mr. Ross replied.

"Mr. Ross, can I ask one simple question?"

"Sure Mark, one question."

"Why so large?"

Mr. Ross smiled as usual and said "Airman." The Airman went over to a box mounted on the wall. It had a large green button that was labeled *Open*, a yellow button labeled *Stop*, and a red button for *Close*. He pushed the green button, and the pod door swung slowly down like the loading ramp on a C130 Hercules cargo plane. Inside the pod was an aircraft.

Mark stood up with a perplexed look on his face, confused but his scientific curiosity had the better of him. Another person may have considered themselves betrayed, but Mark just stood in awe and scientific wonder. "You planned this all along? Were you ever interested in the asteroid strike of sixty-five million years ago?"

Mr. Ross just smiled. "Mark, let's have a look. This is RV1,

Re-Entry Vehicle 1. We plan on doing some time travel. You are going to run the controls and Dom, Maria, and Colonel Jenks are going to be the world's first time travelers."

"Do they know this?" asked Mark. Mark's expression changed from wonder to concern for the safety of his friends. He did however seem a bit relieved that he would be running the controls and was not asked to step into the intimidating craft.

"Of course. Colonel Jenks is an Air Force test pilot. He has flown RV1 many times and is fully prepared for this mission. RV1 has thrusters to operate outside the atmosphere and a conventional jet engine for powered flight within the atmosphere. Dom and Maria are being briefed now so they will understand the importance of the mission. I don't believe they will refuse," replied Mr. Ross.

A moment later, Colonel Jenks entered the room wearing a flight suit, with his helmet in hand. The sergeant followed behind escorting Dom and Maria, who also were in flight suits and carrying helmets. Dom and Maria had blank looks on their faces and were visibly pale and weak-kneed. Dom and Maria both look to Mark, who had the look of concern on his face, and they all acknowledged each other with a forced nervous smile. Each attempting to put one another at ease.

"Sergeant, those items stowed on board?" asked Mr. Ross.

"Yes, sir." The sergeant was trying to move Dom and Maria along gingerly; the rain was really coming down now and there was loud thunder all around them.

The team member that was sent to upload the data was not far behind. "Upload complete, sir," he said to Mr. Ross.

"Thank you young man, dismissed," and he was off.

"Dom and Maria, should we take a little tour of your

ride?" asked Mr. Ross. They managed to nod yes, and the four of them headed to RV1.

Inside RV1 the controls were surprisingly simple, not much different than a modern fighter cockpit, but no co-pilot seat.

"What if something happens to Colonel Jenks with no co-pilot?" asked Maria.

"We have fly-by-wire technology on board. We really don't even need a pilot, we can fly this from right here," replied Mr. Ross.

Dom takes Maria's hand, he can see the concern in her eyes. They both were obviously apprehensive and edgy.

"Maria, although we were basically kidnapped, brought to a super secret military installation in a supersonic craft, were told we are necessary to save the world by traveling in time in an experimental plane, I think the day has gone very well, don't you?" Dom said with dry humor, trying to relieve some of the tension.

Maria laughed and loosened a bit. "Dom, only you could think of something like that in a situation like this," Maria said as she smiled a little less nervously.

"In the event of a complete systems failure, we have back-up systems for environmental control, manual control for propulsion, maneuvering, landing capabilities, and provisions on board for three to last over a week. The ship is designed to withstand the heat of re-entry even in a non-powered landing situation just like the space shuttle. We have lots of extra room because we don't need rocket engines to get us into space like the shuttle does. We will just appear in space," explained Colonel Jenks.

Those were more words than he had spoken all morning, thought Dom.

"For right now we are just going to try things on for size. We are going to power up. Close up the ship and the pod, and everyone get behind the glass," ordered Mr. Ross. Mark and Maria still seemed in shock and were mechanically following orders.

"Remember Dom and Maria, you both did say you wanted to go at the restaurant," joked Mr. Ross. "Dom, I hope I have lived up to the most fantastic adventure you could possibly imagine."

Dom said nervously, "I will never underestimate what you say again."

Mr. Ross squeezed both of their hands with a warm smile and said, "Don't underestimate me now. When it is time for you to go back, I guarantee you will arrive safely. Now buckle up and put on your helmets, it's time to power up the system."

Colonel Jenks already had himself strapped in with his helmet on and gave Mr. Ross the thumbs up on his way out the door.

"Button up that ship and close the door, we are going to power up," ordered Mr. Ross, sounding uncharacteristically military.

It was pitch black inside the ship, with the flat black walls of the pod. Colonel Jenks turned on an internal light.

The cargo-like door swung up and closed, completing the egg shape. Everyone left the

room and the thick glass door was closed.

"Okay, Mark, let's power the system up," said Mr. Ross.

Mark slowly powered up the system to one, then three, then five, then seven. The low-frequency hum was almost deafening and the red glow was so bright that the monitor was difficult to make out as Mark slowly slid the power up to ten. The glass bowed from the gravity and some of the men standing near the glass were pulled toward it.

Inside the ship everything seemed to be in slow motion. Dom tried to speak, but just a low-pitched sound came out. Maria tried to reach for his hand but couldn't seem to move. Then the inside of the pod glowed bright red and then brilliant white.

A loud explosion outside, a white flash of light, and the lab was on fire!

"Power down now!" Ordered Mr. Ross, but the system was already shutting down.

"We are off line," said Mark, still in a bit of shock, but trying to act stoic like Captain Kirk would in the same situation.

"Get in there and get that pod open and get those fires out!" ordered Mr. Ross, again sounding like a military man.

The power was down as they got to the pod. There was a manual crank for an emergency power failure, and they began to crank the door open. It would take some time to open this way, but if they could just get it open enough, they could yell inside to the ship and let them know what was going on.

They got the door open about six inches and looked inside. The pod was empty.

7.

Everyone inside the ship was unconscious.

Jenks revived first. He shook Dom and Maria until they woke.

Dom asked groggily, "How long were we out?"

"According to the ship's mission time clock, looks like we have been out for about five hours."

"Five hours?" said Maria. "How is that possible?"

"I don't know," replied Jenks. "Either of you hurt?"

"No," replied Dom and Maria.

"I guess the system works, look out the window," said Jenks.

"Are we in space?" asked Maria.

"Yes, we are, and that looks like Earth. At least I hope that's

Earth out there in the distance. If it is Earth we should be in its orbital path and it is headed this way very quickly," said Jenks.

The planet was so far away, it was hard to make out, but from what Maria could see there was something a bit odd and the stars didn't look right. "Any of the ship's systems affected?" asked Maria.

"I am running a ship-wide diagnostic right now, but I don't think so. We designed the ship's systems tougher than the probe you tested, so we knew the ship's systems would withstand the jump back."

"You know about the probe?" asked Maria.

"Of course. Who suggested you send back a probe exactly one year in the first place? That's what we all were waiting for. Right after the successful probe test, you were here the next morning. Mr. Ross has been running this project for a very long time," Jenks informed them.

Jenks tried the radio. "RV1 to base, RV1 to base." No response. "We have a locator beacon, they should be in contact soon."

"Assuming we are in the correct century," said Maria.

The planet was approaching very quickly. It looked like the size of Earth, with blue water and cloudy atmosphere. But it had two moons and appeared to be mostly covered in water except for the poles and a land mass coming up on the horizon that they couldn't make out yet.

"We're not in Kansas," said Dom.

"What do you think, Colonel?" asked Maria.

"I think, like it or not, we are going to have to find a way to land there. We can't sit in the vehicle until our provisions are gone. We may need them to survive in our new home, wherever we are."

Jenks hit the thrusters and headed for the planet. As the planet got larger in the window, the land mass came around into view. Dom had a puzzled look on his face. "Maria, do you see those continents down there?"

"Yes, they look very similar to Earth's continents, but too close together to be Earth. Most of what looks something like the United States is under water," said Maria.

Dom replied, "Maria, that *is*,or should I say *will be*, the United States. That's what the continents looked like sixty-five million years ago after the break-up of the supercontinent Pangaea."

"Are you kidding?" asked Jenks.

"No, I am not, Colonel. I am dead serious. I am a paleontologist in addition to being a physicist. I know what I am talking about on those land masses. As far as I know, there was never a second smaller moon in Earth's orbit. But that was sixty-five million years ago; anything could have happened over sixty-five million years. Also, Mark always had minus sixty-five million years come up on his terminal automatically, if someone hit that commit button by accident, this is exactly where we would end up."

"Well you're the expert on this team, any suggestions?" asked Jenks.

Dom replied, "It really doesn't matter where we set down. There is a good chance we are going to be someone's lunch. Every continent on the planet is crawling with the most ferocious predators that ever lived. My best guess is to try to land within walking distance to a mountain range. Maybe we can find a cave to make home and defend. There is one other small issue."

"What's that?" asked Jenks.

"This is just about the time when a six-mile wide asteroid is going to hit in what will be Mexico's Yucatan peninsula."

Maria chimed in, "Let's make the best of this."

"We are going in," said Jenks.

Jenks hit the thrusters but nothing happened. Above them they saw a large space ship pulling them toward it.

"What the heck is that!" yelled Maria.

"It's not one of ours, that's for sure," answered Jenks.

The craft, about the length of two football fields, loomed over them and held them in place. It was a silver blue with odd markings and no apparent engines, radio antennas, or even a bridge that they could see. Its streamlined design was something one would expect for traveling through the atmosphere.

A blue beam of light seemed to slice through RV1 and slowly pan from front to back, causing sparks and small fires along the way. Jenks grabbed the fire extinguisher and put out the flames, but there were too many for him to handle quickly. By the time he got them all out, the electronics systems were down.

"They are pulling us in!" announced Jenks. A large cargo door was opening on the underside of the craft.

Next a red beam sliced through the ship and all three fell unconscious.

8.

When the team awoke, they were lying on what looked like medical examination beds in a bright white room with no windows and no visible door. Jenks tried to sit up first. He realized they were all out of their flight suits and dressed in some kind of pure white jumpsuits. Jenks saw his watch had been removed, so there was no way to tell how long they had been out.

Dom groaned and slowly sat up. Maria sat up after he did.

Jenks asked, "Everyone okay?"

Dom replied first. "Feels like I was doing shots of tequila all night but otherwise okay. How do we turn down that light?"

The light grew visibly dimmer.

Maria said, "A little queasy but fine."

Jenks said, "I wonder who our hosts are?" as he felt the walls with his hand, searching for a seam or a way to open a door.

The ceiling just glowed with white light. There were no light switches or controls, just the three beds in the room. Although they could see no speakers mounted in or on the walls, a female voice seemed to emanate from everywhere: "*Kepspakin*"

"Kepspakin? What language is that?" asked Dom.

Maria replied, "I am no linguist but I don't think that is a word in any language I am aware of."

Jenks tried, "I am Colonel Jenks of the United States Air Force, please identify yourselves and state your intentions."

The voice was heard again: "*god mor*"

"That sounds like English, but I am not sure," said Dom.

"Yes it does a bit, but what does god mor mean?" asked Maria.

"It would be good if we could see each other, that would make communication much easier," said Dom.

"*Good more communication, we will see each other soon,*" the voice announced.

"I think kepspakin means 'keep speaking,' as if they are trying to communicate with us by learning our language. They seem to know the words and are searching for pronunciations. Does that seem possible to you?" said Dom to Maria.

Before Maria could answer the voice came again: "*Yes, good, trying to learn pronunciation.*"

"Wow, they are quick. Who could learn to speak English and its pronunciation that quickly?" said Maria.

"*Tarsi*" was the response.

"Tarsi, who are you and why have you taken us prisoner?" asked Jenks.

"*Not prisoners, we feared our de-con-tam-in-a-tion pro-to-col damaged you and you were brought here for e-val-u-a-tion.*"

"What decontamination protocol are you referring to?" asked Maria, Each exchange with the voice made it more human and less mechanical.

"*Red beam of light.*"

"I remember the red beam coming through the ship just before I passed out," said Maria.

"Yes, I saw it also," said Jenks. "Tarsi, please return us to our ship immediately."

A new male voice responded. "*I am Keevek, of the Tarsi. With deep regret, we have damaged all systems on your ship beyond repair. We did manage to download all data stored in your ship's computer. There is an extensive amount of data stored and we are now analyzing. We first concentrated on your linguistic database to allow us to communicate. The balance will be complete soon, and then we can return you home.*"

"That's impressive. He speaks better English than I do, and why would we have a linguistic database stored on a test flight anyway?" said Dom to the others, then asked "What linguistic database?"

"*Webster's Dictionary. Our system translated English into Tarsi; we understand the words, but we needed a sample of the spoken language to understand the pronunciation reference,*" the voice replied.

"Wow, quick studies," said Dom.

"I have a feeling Mr. Ross once again knew more than he was letting on. I would be curious to see what other extensive data was stored on the ship," said Jenks. "Also, we don't know who we are dealing with here, or where we really are.

We may not be back in time, and this could be a hostile race looking for our planet's location, so let's not give them any more information than we have to. Let's minimize the information we give them to what intel they have already captured. Until we can determine otherwise, we have to assume we have been attacked and they are a hostile race."

"We are not hostile; would you please proceed to the briefing room by following the green line?" At that moment a doorway seemed to dematerialize in front of them and a green line appeared on the floor. All Maria could manage was "Wow."

Jenks said, "Why not, but keep the info exchange to a minimum, understood?"

Dom and Maria nodded yes. They stepped out into the hallway that seemed just the right size for humans, almost what you would expect on a cruise ship. But the hallway looked like the room they were just in: smooth white illuminated walls, but with a pronounced green line leading the way. They followed the green line through several turns until they saw an opening in a wall ahead. Cautiously, with Jenks leading the way, they stepped inside.

Maria had such a grip on Dom's arm she was close to cutting off the circulation. Although Dom was scared stiff, he didn't show it and was quite content to let her hang on. Inside the room there was a large somewhat oval table, jet black, and black chairs around the table. "Guess they are not big on color in their décor," commented Dom.

"Please sit and make yourselves comfortable," a voice piped in. This time it was a different, female voice.

There was a pitcher of water, glasses, and a bowl of fruit on the table; none of the fruit was recognizable to them.

Dom reached for a fruit that looked like an oversized pear but was orange. Jenks stopped him. "Dom, don't eat or drink anything yet until we understand more." Dom complied.

Two Tarsi entered the room. They were slightly shorter than the average adult human male, about 5 feet 6 inches tall, but very muscular, with dark black eyes, no hair, and heads slightly larger than a human head. Their most striking feature was teeth. They had mouths larger than a human mouth, filled with what appeared to be very sharp teeth. The sight was intimidating at first.

Dom thought, *I knew we would be someone's lunch.*

One of the Tarsi spoke. "I am Keevek, of the Tarsi. Welcome to Tarsi City," he said in perfect English.

"Tarsi City? We are no longer on the ship?" inquired Jenks.

"No, you were all sleeping for some time, six hours in your terms, and in that time you were brought here. Dom, you will not be our lunch, please do not be concerned," replied Keevek.

"I only thought that. How did you know what I was thinking?" asked Dom.

"We have on occasion a capacity to hear the thoughts of others. Some of our race is very accomplished at this, while others cannot communicate in this fashion very well. And in response to your other thought, yes, we are descended from a dinosaur similar to what you call a velociraptor. We have evolved into omnivores, and can process plant material as food as well as meat," replied Keevek.

"I am C'net of the Tarsi," the other Tarsi said in a female voice. "We have finished analyzing the data retrieved from your computer system, and your superior has some specific instructions for you and the Tarsi as well."

"For the Tarsi as well? This has to be from Mr. Ross," said Jenks.

"The instructions are quite specific, we are to give you instructions at specific times from when you arrived," said C'Net.

"We are now confirming the research done by Miss D'Luce. If it is correct, you are messengers sent here to save the entire Tarsi race. You will be considered heroes by all Tarsi," stated Keevek.

"What message?" asked Jenks.

Maria started, "The asteroid that will hit the Earth and wipe out almost all life."

Keevek closed his eyes as if in thought. "I have just received confirmation. Based on data and research Miss D'Luce collected, we knew where to look. There is in fact a six-mile-wide asteroid that will strike Tarsi City in 1.5 orbits or years. Based on your message, we will have time to evacuate all Tarsi." Keevek pointed to the white wall and a map of the Earth was projected with perfect clarity. "This is where Tarsi City is located." He pointed to the Yucatan peninsula of Mexico, a red dot was projected on the map. "This is where the asteroid will strike." Another dot was projected directly on top of the city. "Tarsi City will be vaporized and as you have referenced in some of your literature, we are at ground zero," concluded Keevek.

"Don't you have any kind of technology that can deflect the asteroid?" asked Maria.

"The city is surrounded by an energy barrier strong enough to keep out the wildlife, but not strong enough to protect us from the asteroid. As far as moving the asteroid, it is moving too fast, has too much mass, and is too close for us to deflect it enough to save the city. We must evacuate. This has happened many times before. 185 million orbits or years ago, 250 million years ago from your time reference, another large asteroid struck Rahn, which you call Earth. That asteroid extinguished almost all life on the planet. This was fortuitous for the Tarsi because if this had not occurred, the Tarsi most likely would not have evolved. Likewise for humans, if this asteroid does not strike, or if we could deflect the asteroid, most likely humans will not evolve, and you would not return as emissaries from a different time to warn us. Our peoples are linked in time and dependent on each other," replied C'Net.

"Are there any other cities on the planet?" asked Dom.

"No, all the Tarsi are located in Tarsi City. Tarsi City is quite large, approximately 100 miles in diameter, and millions of Tarsi live here. The rest of the planet is dominated by the dinosaurs," replied C'Net.

"I guess that makes sense. That is why no evidence of the Tarsi was ever found; all that will be left is Chicxulub crater," said Dom.

"That is correct, and we will be making some effort to make sure nothing is ever found. That is part of the instruction set I am authorized to reveal to you," stated C'Net.

"We have finished analyzing your medical and human biological data and have determined what foods you can safely consume. You all must replenish yourselves and retire to your quarters. All Tarsi would like to offer thanks to you tomorrow. So please eat and we will show you to your quarters," concluded C'Net as she walked through the opening, gesturing for them to follow.

"Why not, we have nowhere else to go," said Jenks.

"All Tarsi? They must have one heck of an Internet," said Maria.

9.

Colonel Jenks awoke early; the bed he slept in was the most comfortable bed he had ever slept in. It automatically adjusted temperature and firmness to suit its occupant, optimizing sleep time.

When he got out of bed, there was a new opening in his quarters leading to a bathroom with a shower, sink, and modern toilet. Apparently Mr. Ross had included the design in the data stored on RVI in anticipation of their stay.

On a small table against the wall was a leather bag with the name *Colonel Jenks* on the side. Jenks unzipped the bag and on top there was a letter with bright red lettering *For Colonel Jenks Eyes Only*, stamped *Top Secret* and instructions

Open Upon Arrival. Jenks picked up the envelope, it had the presidential seal. He opened the letter. It read:

Colonel Jenks, if you are reading this you have arrived in an unexpected place and time.

There are other letters attached to a package in the bottom of your bag. Under no circumstances are you to open the other letters or the package until you arrive back at your projected time on Earth.

You must keep your bag and package with you on your mission to your projected time of arrival. This may seem vague and confusing now, but in time you will understand completely.

This is a direct order. Best of luck on your mission and Godspeed.

Signed President George W. Bush

Yes, sir, thought Jenks with a perplexed expression on his face. *He's right; I am confused. I wonder what my mission is?* Inside the bag were some casual clothing, towels, and toiletries. Jenks grabbed a towel and some soap and stepped to the shower, it had no controls. *Interesting*, thought Jenks. *I wonder how they could have overlooked a detail like that?* He stepped into the shower and the water automatically came on at the perfect temperature. *Should have known better than to doubt*, thought Jenks. Jenks finished his shower, put on some of the clothes, which were a perfect fit, and looked for an exit. There was no door in the room.

He spoke out loud, "Where's the mess?" A door appeared in the wall and he heard the words "*Please proceed to the mess by following the green line.*"

Should have known, thought Jenks.

Jenks followed the green line to an opening in the wall. He stepped inside to a café-like setting. There were several tables, many of them with Tarsi sitting at them.

The Tarsi looked up and made a sort of nod and bow, almost like a Japanese bow. Several Tarsi he walked by made the same gesture. A wash of emotion came over him, it was a feeling of gratitude, welcome, and respect.

Jenks suddenly felt very comfortable. He smiled and awkwardly returned the gesture. Dom, Maria, and C'Net were already sitting at a table. C'Net spoke first. "Welcome. Did you sleep well, Colonel Jenks?"

Jenks replied "Yes, very well, thank you."

Maria said, "You look good in your civvies, Colonel. I see you had luggage delivered to your room as well."

Dom was unusually energetic this morning, holding a clear glass full of a steaming-hot purple liquid that appeared thicker than water. "Colonel, you have to try this drink. I was jonesing for a cup of coffee, and C'Net suggested I try this. It's incredible! I'm good to go!" said Dom, obviously feeling the effects of the drink.

"Slow down there cowboy," replied Jenks. "I'm thinking that has a bit more kick than coffee." Jenks was actually loosening up a bit.

There were fruits, a plate of white cooked meat, and something that looked like bread but with a red tint. "Your biological systems are compatible with all of the Tarsi foods. Feel free to try whatever appeals to you," stated C'Net.

"Try the meat, try the meat! Bet you can't guess what it tastes like! It tastes like chicken but it's ornithomimus! I actually ate ornithomimus!" said Dom, talking faster than normal.

Colonel Jenks actually chuckled. "Dom, I think you better water down that purple stuff you are drinking. I think it's espresso times ten. C'Net, is that caffeine in that drink Dom has?"

"Yes, there is. We will adjust the caffeine level in the drink for you in the future," replied C'Net.

"Good idea," replied Jenks.

Maria asked, "C'Net, how long has the Tarsi civilization been in existence?"

C'Net replied, "We began recording our history approximately 1.5 million orbits ago."

"How many Tarsi are there in Tarsi City?" asked Jenks.

"There are 2.315 million Tarsi in Tarsi City," replied C'Net.

"Only 2.315 million? That seems like a small number for a one-and-a-half-million-year-old civilization," Dom blurted out.

"In the beginning, many Tarsi were killed by the dinosaur predators. Our numbers were down to several thousand. What were left of us migrated here, to this location, where we constructed shelters that could protect us from the predators. Here we all have remained since. In addition, compared to mammalian standards, we reproduce slowly, and in small numbers, usually one or two, but sometimes three offspring per pairing."

"Do you have any children, C'Net?" asked Maria.

"No, I have not chosen a male for pairing as yet. I am still a bit young and have much to learn before I am ready to raise young."

"May I ask how old you are?"

"I am fifty-one orbits or years old," replied C'Net.

"Fifty-one years and you are too young? How long do most Tarsi live?" asked Maria in surprise.

"The average lifespan of a Tarsi ranges from three hundred and seventy-five to four hundred orbits. There are ways to extend this span if the individual Tarsi so chooses, and some do, but most choose to go naturally, after their body begins to fail," answered C'Net.

"I guess I can understand that, if I was around four hundred years old I guess I would be ready to check out too," said Jenks.

"Imagine what the human race could accomplish working together as a team, with a common goal and a lifespan and maturity of four hundred years of life," said Dom, speaking much more slowly and calming down.

"If you all are finished, would you like a tour of the city?" asked C'Net.

"We are all ready, I believe," said Jenks. C'Net placed her hand on the table, said a word in Tarsi, and the table was suddenly clear and spotless.

"I have got to get one of these tables," said Dom, and they headed outside.

10.

As they were walking down the long white hallway C'Net started, "The system is now ready to accept all your requests in English. You need only speak as to where you would like to go and the system will show you the way. We are headed to the courtyard. Dom would you like to try?"

Dom spoke, "I want to go to the courtyard." A green line appeared on the floor and the system spoke, "*Please proceed to the courtyard by following the green line.*"

"This will work anywhere in Tarsi City, so no matter where you are you will always be able to find your way," explained C'Net.

"Cool," said Dom.

It looked like C'Net smiled, but it was hard to tell. "Also, your rooms will respond to the system in an intuitive fashion. If you request 75 degrees, it will know you mean 75 degrees Fahrenheit and not 75 degrees centigrade."

The wall opened as they approached the end of the hall and they all stepped out into the courtyard; there was an immediate feeling of acceptance and warmth as they stepped out, much stronger than in the café.

There were thousands of Tarsi there and Dom thought it felt as if they were all there to meet them. Every Tarsi they walked by did the sort of nod-bow to show their respect. There was a long line of Tarsi waiting their turn to view a glass case. As they approached, they saw RV1, encased in what appeared to be a thick clear plastic, and thousands of Tarsi were waiting their turn patiently to get a glimpse. "The Tarsi are here to greet you. The ones that could not fit on the promenade are telepathically sending their thanks, so you will feel their gratitude," explained C'Net.

"Wow, we are rock stars," said Dom.

The sky was a clear blue, without clouds, and there was kind of a shimmering to the sky as they looked up. "What is that shimmering in the sky?" asked Maria.

"That is the energy barrier that protects Tarsi City from the predators and dinosaurs from wandering through. It has provided us safety and allowed us to flourish for nearly a million years." The buildings were tall and ornate. They were all constructed from what appeared to be polished white marble and glass, but when the humans touched them, it felt more like plastic.

"The ancient Romans and Greeks had nothing on these guys," said Dom.

"How can you build these buildings so tall out of this stone material?" asked Maria.

"The material is a synthetic stone. It is stronger than titanium but much easier to work with. In the case of one of the taller buildings, we simply dampen the local gravity field, lessening the burden to its structural members. Then we add gravity to each floor. There is actually no limit as to how tall we could build the buildings, but we keep them to a maximum height just for convenience," replied C'Net.

"Dampen the local gravity field?" asked Maria.

"Yes, it is similar technology to how we propel our spacecraft. We use a gravity drive and simply push ourselves where we want to go. I apologize but gravity manipulation is not one of my areas of expertise. If you like, I could introduce you to Professor Seeri, she could explain in detail," stated C'Net.

"Maybe some other time. I think we are all pretty curious about the city for now," replied Jenks. Both Dom and Maria nodded in agreement.

"Perhaps we should start with The Repository of Tarsi History. This will give you a good basis and reference for understanding the Tarsi," suggested C'Net.

"Sounds good," the humans all chimed together.

Dom said, "Turn off the audio for directions and show me the way to The Repository of Tarsi History." Silently the green line appeared down the promenade and ended about 1,000 feet away at a stately building with what looked like pillars from the Acropolis. It had hieroglyphs above the door shaped like triangles, lines, and circles with lines through them, and one that looked like a fish hook.

"Are those glyphs the Tarsi written language?" asked Maria.

"Yes. It reads 'The Repository of Tarsi History,'" replied C'Net.

"That makes sense," said Dom.

C'Net smiled somewhat again and asked, "I am trying to understand your humor. Is statement of the obvious and literal interpretation considered humorous in your culture?"

"Yes, sometimes, C'Net. But done too often it would not be," replied Maria.

"I believe I understand," said C'Net.

"Walk this way," said Dom as he started down the green line. C'Net got behind him and tried to imitate his gait. The humans all burst out laughing.

"He said walk this way," said C'Net.

"I believe you are getting it, C'Net. Were there any Stooges videos stored on the ship?" asked Maria.

"Stooges?" inquired C'Net with a puzzled look.

"Never mind," said Maria.

They followed the green line to the repository. As they walked, any Tarsi standing even near their path stepped aside and bowed respectfully. As they reached the front of the building, Tarsi were in a long line waiting to get in, each one nodding in reverence as they passed, but none of them were standing on the green line for fear of blocking its view from their visitors. The green line went up the front stairs to the front of the building and ended.

As they approached the front of the building a typical Tarsi opening was already there. The inside was set up in a circular path. As they followed the path counterclockwise the exhibits got progressively more advanced. "This is like visiting a museum of natural history back in our time," Maria commented. The first exhibit was of several Tarsi with crude weapons, fighting off a pack of velociraptors and defending a cave home.

The second exhibit showed Tarsi who had constructed an enclosure of rock walls and dwellings of rock and mud that offered better protection from the predators. About halfway around, the exhibit showed a modest Tarsi city, nowhere near the size of the city

as it was now but with the shimmering energy field covering it like a transparent dome. "Is this the beginning of the use of the energy shield?" asked Jenks.

"Yes, the energy shield was first deployed 953 thousand orbits ago. The version you see here is crude by comparison to the shield we use now, but it was quite effective in keeping us safe from the dinosaurs."

"Those exhibits seem so real and lifelike. Are we allowed to touch them?" asked Maria.

"The exhibits are not solid objects. You would call them holograms," replied C'Net. A bit further up was an exhibit of a Tarsi scientist with an object floating in the air. C'Net read the glyphs: "The first gravity dampening field."

Shortly after that exhibit, the Tarsi City buildings dwarfed the previous buildings in height. Near the end of the exhibit there was a display of Dom, Colonel Jenks, and Maria standing in front of RV1 in the courtyard, with C'Net, Keevek, and Maria pointing to the sky.

Dom, Maria, and the Colonel look at each other in amazement. "You have included an exhibit of us in the repository?" said Dom stating the obvious.

"Yes, of course, you are now a significant part of Tarsi history, and the message you have delivered will impact the lives of all Tarsi now living and every Tarsi yet to exist." Replied C'Net.

Included in the exhibit was a small representation of the solar system out to the Ort cloud and a globe of the Earth with the two moons orbiting and the asteroid approaching.

C'Net asked, "Dom may I ask you a question?"

Dom replied, "Sure C'Net, anything."

"We were hoping you could help us with your astronomical reference. We assumed it had some significance where you kept it with you, but our astronomers and even the system could not relate it to any of our astronomical references."

Dom looked puzzled. "What astronomical reference do you mean? I didn't know I had any astronomical reference with me."

"On your back. 'Ort iz 34.' Is that not a sector in the Ort cloud?" asked C'Net.

Dom smiled and replied, "No. I am sorry you spent so much time on that, C'Net. In our culture we play games comprised of teams; each team, depending on the game, has varying numbers of players. The shirt I wear bears the name and numerical designation of one of those players."

"What is the game called?" asked C'Net.

"Baseball, and my shirt represents the greatest team in baseball and the most clutch player in baseball history."

"Would you be willing to explain the game to us at some point?" asked C'Net.

Maria groaned playfully and said, "Be careful, C'Net. If you get him going on baseball, it's hard to stop him."

"I will use caution, Maria," said C'Net, smiling the best she could.

Maria spoke up. "C'Net, in all the excitement I forgot to bring this up. In our time there is only one moon."

C'Net replied, "I believe the next and last exhibit will explain."

As they walked to the last exhibit the humans were awed; there were thousands of Tarsi working in space around the smaller moon. C'Net continued, "We call the moons Rahn sub 1 and Rahn sub 2. Rahn sub 2 is mostly iron and rock, materials easily manipulated into materials needed to construct a transport large enough to hold all Tarsi, crops, and livestock on an extended journey. Rahn sub 2 will be completely harvested, and with some materials from Rahn and Rahn sub 1, or the Moon, we will have the transport done in time. As you can see, construction has already begun."

"Already begun? How could you have started so quickly?" asked Jenks.

C'Net replied, "The system provided the design, and we already manufacture most of our larger crafts in orbit now. We regularly harvest iron asteroids for raw materials from space, so it was a simple matter to have our manufacturing facility begin processing material from Rahn sub 2 into structural members. Our calculations show there will not be quite enough material from Rahn sub 2 to complete the transport, so this answers the question for your time. Rahn sub 2 will be completely harvested. We will also have to dismantle parts of Tarsi City to complete the project."

"Where did you find so many Tarsi to work on this so quickly?" asked Jenks.

"Since Tarsi City will end in 1.5 orbits, there were many projects no longer necessary and were discontinued. In the coming days and months, more and more Tarsi and resources will be devoted to the project," stated C'Net.

C'Net asked if they had any additional questions. Dom replied, "About a million, but I would like to see more of the city before nightfall if we could."

"Of course. Would you like to view Tarsi City from the sky?"

"Sounds great," replied Jenks.

11.

They walked out of the Repository and headed to the back of the building. Parked there were several vehicles with open tops of various sizes. C'Net chose one that could seat all four and everyone climbed in.

"Can anyone use these?" asked Maria.

C'Net replied, "Yes, the vehicles are available for any Tarsi who needs one. There are usually several stored behind most of the larger buildings, although most Tarsi walk to their destinations within the center. The vehicles are used quite often by those who work on the outer edges of the city but who have business to conduct in the center."

"This can fly?" asked Jenks.

"Is that humor?" asked C'Net.

"No, sorry." Jenks replied.

"Please pull the safety device forward when you are seated comfortably," requested C'Net. The control was a ball seemingly floating in the air over C'Net.

"How does that work?" asked Jenks.

C'Net replied, "This is a three dimensional control device. If I pull up on the ball, we will rise; if I push down we'll land. Likewise for any direction on the x-y-z axis I wish to travel to, I simply move the ball in that direction. The more force I put on the ball in that direction, the faster we will travel. It has built-in safety features that prevent descending too quickly, or colliding with buildings or other objects."

"Let's go," said Maria.

C'Net pulled up on the control and they ascended straight up over the top of the buildings. Next she pushed slightly forward, and the vehicle headed off.

They were in the center of Tarsi City, and it was a clear day so they could see quite some distance to the agricultural areas. C'Net flew them over the center of the city pointing out some of the more significant structures. The first building they flew over was the Consortium of Science and Research. "This is where the best scientific minds work together to develop technologies needed to improve the Tarsi way of life." The next building was Health and Medical Research Center. C'Net said, "Some of the Tarsi words do not translate exactly into English. I hope you will accept my interpretation."

"You are doing great," said Jenks. He continued, "C'Net, I am sure I speak for all of us when I say we appreciate the time you are taking with us. I hope we are not keeping you from other pressing matters. I am sure you have other things to do rather than spend your day with the three of us in tow."

C'Net looked a bit surprised by the Colonel's comment. "Colonel Jenks, thousands of Tarsi requested this honor. Keevek and I were fortunate enough to greet you, but I was chosen to orient you to our civilization and culture. This is the most important event in Tarsi history, and I was chosen. I hope I am providing adequate service to you all."

"Yes, of course you are. We were concerned for you because we didn't want to inconvenience you, that is what the Colonel meant," explained Maria.

C'Net smiled. "One of the reasons I was chosen was for my sense of humor, and by Tarsi standards, I am considered quite entertaining."

"Wow, Tarsi comedians must play some tough rooms," Dom chimed in.

C'Net smiled and half-laughed. "Yes, tough rooms." She sort of chuckled as she spoke.

They were flying toward the northern boundary of the energy barrier. Dom looked down at what appeared to be a grass pasture. The grass was a much darker green than usual, and below there were animals running in groups. "Is that grass?" asked Maria.

Dom replied, "Maria, grass was thought to evolve somewhere between sixty-five and one hundred million years ago, so there is a good chance it is similar to the grass we have back in our time."

"Correct. However, this grass has been enriched with nutrients. The air has a higher carbon dioxide content than the air in your time. Plants grow much faster but have a lower nutritional value. We enrich the plants inside the energy barrier to be much more nutritious than those outside, for both our livestock and for our own consumption," C'Net said.

"Can we go lower?" asked Dom. C'Net took the vehicle down.

"We cannot go too low, the ornithomimus can jump quite high, and being omnivores, they can be dangerous."

"Wow, actual living ornithomimus, and look they are covered in small feathers. I knew it! I wish I had a video recorder now!" said Dom. "C'Net, are the ornithomimus warm-blooded?"

"Yes, in fact all dinosaurs living in what you refer to the Cretaceous are warm-blooded."

Dom was getting very excited to see the live dinosaurs. "Is there somewhere we can set down to get a better look?"

"If you like we can set down in the hadrosaurus enclosure. They are easily startled and will run, but otherwise are not dangerous. We can set down near the edge of the barrier. That way you can examine the grass, and look outside the barrier."

"Look over there, hadrosaurus!" exclaimed Dom. Both Jenks and Maria couldn't help smiling at Dom's childlike glee.

They set the vehicle down near the northernmost border of the energy field. There were a flock of hadrosaurus about 1,000 feet away nibbling on ferns and grass. The hadrosaurus looked for a time, decided the four were not a threat, and with casual disregard continued grazing.

Jenks knelt down to feel the grass, "Not exactly Kentucky Bluegrass. A little coarse, but otherwise I wouldn't mind my lawn looking this good."

Dom had the wide eyes of a child. He couldn't take it all in quickly enough. First he watched the hadrosaurus, and then turned his attention to outside the barrier. "Look, Maria! Look at all the flowers! I knew there were flowering plants, but I had no idea they would be so diverse. And look, horsetails, Williamsonia, conifers, seed ferns—Maria, can you believe it!" Dom exclaimed as he approached the barrier.

"Dom, there is no danger. You can approach the barrier and can even touch it. But be warned, you could be startled if a predator sees you because it may run into the barrier," warned C'Net.

"Okay, thanks, C'Net," Dom replied as he moved closer. He reached up and touched the barrier; it felt like a thick plastic and if pushed on, it would move slightly, but the harder he pushed the more solid it became. "This is incredible." He paused. "Is that a velociraptor behind that fern, C'Net?"

"Not exactly, Dom. It is very similar, and as far as we can tell it is indigenous to only this local area. They are very similar to velociraptors in many ways, but significantly more aggressive and intelligent. They are our genetic cousins and they have a strong sense of commitment to their pack. They instinctively work for the common good of the pack, a trait inherited by the Tarsi, and nearly wiped out the early Tarsi. As you saw in the repository, we have been defending ourselves from them for a long time. The velociraptors you speak of have been gone for nearly 20 million years. In fact, there are many types of unique dinosaurs that only live in the immediate area around the energy shield. For reasons we have not completely determined, the shield attracts predators, and these particular predators arrived in greater numbers shortly after we first energized the shield."

"Of course. I should have known that the original velociraptors would have been extinct, but caught up in this excitement, I forgot the timeline."

Dom was nearly pressing his face to the shield straining to get a better look at the raptor. Out of the corner of his eye he saw another raptor eight feet in the air coming down with the huge claws on its feet aimed right at him. He fell back on his backside in reflex. The raptor hit the shield and bounced off; six other raptors he hadn't seen before were rushing at the same time. The raptor got up and shook his head as if in disbelief at the easy meal he lost. They all turned and disappeared into the vegetation as quickly as they had come out.

"Whoa," said Dom.

"You were never in any real danger, but it can be unnerving when they attack the shield. The hadrosaurus have learned to ignore them. The older raptors no longer attack the shield since they have learned that they cannot penetrate. The younger ones try, but learn quickly," explained C'Net.

"That was an amazing display of intelligence. One of the raptors drew my attention, while the others formed an organized attack plan working together. I wouldn't want to meet them outside the shield," stated Dom, still lying on his back.

"No, I should think not," said C'Net.

Maria rushed over to help Dom up. "Are you all right?"

"Yes, fine, thank you. Just a little shaken. It's not every day one of the most ferocious and cunning predators that ever lived comes within two feet of tearing you to shreds," replied Dom, his eyes wide with scientific interest. "Now I know firsthand how their prey felt, something no other paleontologist could ever hope to know. It was an amazing experience."

Jenks chuckled. "Dom, only a true dinosaur geek could say something like that after having one of those things launched at him."

Dom grinned and got to his feet, still shaking a bit. Maria was holding his hand, and his attention quickly shifted to her.

At that moment Jenks shouted in pain. A fanged lizard about a foot long was running away. Blood stained Jenks' thigh, he tore open his pant leg to see two puncture wounds.

C'Net looked concerned and said, "We must head back to the city immediately."

"It's no big deal. It was just a small bite. He was an aggressive little guy, wasn't he?"

"Colonel Jenks, that is a cleaner lizard we have engineered for pest control. It feeds on the small mammals that eat our crops. It is venomous, bites its prey, and then watches from a distance until the venom does its work. After its prey dies, it comes to feed without risk of injury. The venom is a powerful neurotoxin that will begin to take effect quickly. I apologize. It feeds exclusively on mammals and it must have recognized you as a food source."

"My hands and feet are getting numb and I feel a little light-headed," Jenks said, looking concerned.

"The neurotoxin begins in the extremities and will eventually stop your heart. Please get in the vehicle now."

12.

Colonel Jenks was a bit shaky getting into the vehicle; he had begun to sweat and small red lines were visible radiating from the bite area since he had torn open his pants. C'Net spoke in Tarsi, "Health and Medical Research Center, medical emergency." The vehicle took over automatically and sped toward the city.

The poison progressed quickly while they were in flight. The red lines spread down Jenks' leg to his foot and he had trouble holding his head up. When they arrived at the hospital, four Tarsi greeted them at the front door with a floating stretcher. With some help from Dom and Maria, Jenks managed to get out of the vehicle. Placing one arm over Dom's shoulder and one over Maria's shoulder, he climbed onto the stretcher.

They rushed Colonel Jenks into a treatment room and placed him on an evaluation bed. His vitals were displayed on the white wall in both Tarsi and English. Immediately, the system spoke: "*Blood pressure 90 over 50 and falling pulse 38, normal range for human physiology are 120 over 80 and pulse 65 immediate intervention required*"

"We must administer the serum," Doctor Teek said.

"We don't know the long-term effect of the serum on human physiology," another doctor objected. "It has never been used on a mammalian before!"

Jenks was in visible distress, having difficulty breathing and writhing in pain.

Maria held the Colonel's hand compassionately. Dom tried to hold the Colonel down to keep him from injuring himself.

Doctor Teek asked the system, "Projected time before expiration of subject?"

The system responded first in Tarsi then in English, "*17 minutes; effective treatment window 10 minutes*"

Maria gasped and had a terrified look on her face. Dom was having some trouble holding Colonel Jenks down, he was very strong, and the agony he was in made him even stronger. "I know it's hard, but try not to fall off the table Colonel," Dom advised the Colonel compassionately.

Jenks managed to say, "Give it to me now. There won't be anything to discuss in ten minutes."

Doctor Teek picked up a vial of the clear serum and placed it on Jenks' forearm; the serum just seemed to drain from the vial into Jenks.

For the first minute nothing seemed to happen, and

then Jenks' pulse started to increase and his blood pressure started to rise.

Doctor Teek looked somewhat relieved, but was cautiously watching the monitor for vital signs, not exactly sure what to expect.

Maria took a deep breath and released a sigh of relief. Dom dropped to the floor in exhaustion from trying to contain Colonel Jenks.

He was breathing a little more easily. After a moment, he said shakily, "I am feeling better … pain is going … what was in that stuff?"

Doctor Teek responded, "There are many plant and animal components to the serum. Some of them include crocodilian antibodies, to boost the immune system, Tarsi antibodies, and several plant and animal extracts you would not be familiar with."

The red lines were fading, and Jenks looked visibly better. Doctor Teek said, "I suggest Colonel Jenks remain here for observation for the time being. For the moment he is out of trouble, but we just do not know how his system will react to the serum over the next few hours."

"I have no problem with that. I could use some shut-eye anyway. Thank you doctors, you did a great job," replied Jenks.

"You are most welcome, it was our honor to serve you," they replied in unison.

"How did the system adapt to our physiology so quickly?" asked Maria.

"While you were in flight, we have had the system calibrate our instruments to interpret human physiology, it was a simple process and the data we needed was stored on your ship," Doctor Teek explained.

"Ross again," mutterer the Colonel.

"You should all leave now, and let Colonel Jenks get some rest," suggested Doctor Teek.

"Can't we stay with Colonel Jenks for a while?" asked Maria.

Doctor Teek had a concerned look on his face, not wanting to start conflict with Maria, but sincerely wished them to leave the Colonel to rest.

Dom sensing this said, "I think we will head to the café if C'Net and Maria are okay with that. Do you want me to bring you back a hadrosaurus burger or something, Colonel?"

"No, thanks, Dom. I think I will just get some sleep and I will see you in the morning." The colonel closed his eyes and was asleep almost as soon as his eyes shut.

No one really noticed before, but C'Net was really shaken up. She'd almost gotten one of the human heroes killed just now. Dom, sensing her emotions tried to cheer her up. "You know C'Net, that event was completely unpredictable. There was nothing you could have done better. Because of you, the Colonel is safe and resting comfortably. Also, if it were not for you, I would never have known about the purple drink. I can't wait for your next recommendation." C'Net and Maria both laugh.

"Man, I could really go for a cheese pizza and a coffee with extra extra," said Dom.

C'Net replied, "We have analyzed the data of your typical foodstuffs and we now have had enough time to experiment. I believe we can get fairly close to the foods you are accustomed to eating. Unfortunately, no color reference was given, so they may not look like what you are used to seeing, but the taste and texture should be close."

"That's amazing, C'Net. I ate ornithomimus for breakfast, so I guess I can try Tarsi pizza," Dom replied.

"Maria, what would you like?" asked C'Net.

"I think I would like a salad with Italian dressing, carbonated water, and a piece of garlic bread," replied Maria.

When they arrived at the café their food was waiting for them. Dom's pizza had a deep red crust and the topping was a rich green, like the color of the grass they had just been on. His coffee was also green. Dom picked up a slice. "Here goes." He took a bite, and his eyes widened. "This is great pizza, what is it made of?"

C'Net replied, "Grasses, grains, lactose, plant gum, animal fat…"

Dom cut her off. "Thanks C'Net, I don't want to know the rest. I don't want to spoil it." He tried his coffee and exclaimed, "This is the best green coffee I ever had. Maria, C'Net, do you want to try a slice?"

Maria declined, but C'Net picked up a slice and took a bite.

"Very tasty and spicy; I like it," C'Net commented.

Maria tried her salad; it was a deep green, but not leafy like lettuce. It looked more like the grass they had seen. She reluctantly took a bite, and smiled. "This is very good. Thank you C'Net."

C'Net smiled and said, "You are welcome."

"C'Net, what do the Tarsi do in their leisure time? What are your forms of entertainment?" asked Dom.

"We have many forms of entertainment. We enjoy swimming, the observatory on Rahn sub 1, and orb matches, to name a few."

"Orb matches?"

"Orb matches are played on a grass field with two teams of six Tarsi each. One Tarsi from each team protects the orb receptor, then the other five attempt to kick the orb into the opposing team's receptor. The challenge is the players may not use their hands, only their feet; it is a very fast-paced game and quite popular."

"Soccer! We have a similar game we play called soccer. There are more players on each team, but it sounds basically the same. Could we see an orb match?" asked Dom.

"Unfortunately, orb matches have been suspended since all available Tarsi are now working on the evacuation of Tarsi City. However, if you wish to view a match, simply ask the system to display a recorded match for you when you retire to your quarters," explained C'Net.

"Maria, look how advanced they are and they still have cable and re-runs. If we ever get back, remind me to invest in cable TV," joked Dom.

Maria asked, "C'Net, could we visit the observatory?"

"Why, yes, of course. I believe tomorrow would be a good day. I do not feel Colonel Jenks would enjoy the observatory as much as you and Dom, and while he is resting and recovering tomorrow, this could be an ideal time."

"Wait a minute; you said the observatory was on Rahn sub 1. We would have to go to the moon to visit the observatory?" asked Dom with some concern.

"Yes, Dom, the best place to observe the universe is above

the atmosphere. I believe you would find the visit quite informative and interesting," C'Net explained.

"I guess we are off to the moon tomorrow," said Dom.

Maria was visibly energized; she looked a bit like a young child that was going to Disney World tomorrow for the first time. "Dom what an opportunity, to look at the universe as it was sixty-five million years ago! I am so excited; how will I sleep?"

Dom smiled a warm smile and put his hand over hers.

"Dom, perhaps after you observe one of the orb matches you would explain baseball to me?" requested C'Net.

Maria said, "C'Net, you don't know what you have done." C'Net smiled; she was smiling much less awkwardly after observing Dom, Maria, and Jenks. And she knew Maria was playing with Dom.

Dom replied, "I would love to, but if the Tarsi ever take up baseball, I want to be the first manager. I will change my name to Francona and manage the team called the Boston Red Sox." Maria rolled her eyes playfully.

C'Net recognized that Dom was making a joke; she chuckled a bit and said, "Sounds like an equitable trade, Dom."

Maria finished her salad and announced, "C'Net, thank you for a wonderful day. I would like to return to my quarters and get some rest for tomorrow. Dom, will you walk with me?"

No sooner had she finished speaking than Dom stood up to join her. C'Net made a respectful bow and Dom and Maria were off.

As Dom and Maria were walking, Dom asked, "Maria, do you think it would be okay if we stopped by to see how

Colonel Jenks is doing before we turn in?" Maria nodded yes and took Dom's hand.

They walked to the Health and Medical Research Center. Dom spoke out loud, "Please show the way to Colonel Jenks Room," the familiar green line appeared. Standing in the hallway outside Colonel Jenks' room, Dom asked the system, "Could we please see Colonel Jenks?"

The system responded *"Colonel Jenks is now sleeping. Doctor Teek has instructed that Colonel Jenks not be disturbed unless medically necessary; however, his vital signs and observation window are now provided"* A clear window-like opening appeared in the wall; his vital statistics were blood pressure 120/80 and pulse 59, his color was back to normal, and he appeared to be resting comfortably.

Dom said, "Maria, let's head back. It looks like Colonel Jenks is doing much better; we can stop by in the morning to see how he is progressing."

Maria smiled, impressed that Dom had so much concern for Colonel Jenks. "That's nice that you care so much about how he is doing."

Dom replied, "He isn't what I expected based on our first meeting. He was cold and distant, but he has really come around. There is just something about him that makes me feel he is a real stand-up guy, that you can trust and rely on him."

Maria nodded as if in agreement.

They walked, holding hands, back to Maria's quarters without saying a word. Outside Maria's door, Dom said, "Good night."

As he turned to walk away, Maria grabbed him by the shirt, pulled him toward her, and kissed him. "If I waited for you to do that, we would have been old and gray," she said with a smile, and then instructed the door to close.

Dom stood there with his mouth hanging open a bit, a stunned expression on his face. Then slowly, a wide grin appeared and he started toward his quarters.

His quarters had been cleaned and organized and a bowl of fruit had been placed on his table. He picked up one of the orange pears, sat on his bed, and said, "I would like to see the last orb match played."

The field was displayed on the wall. It looked to be about twice the size of a normal soccer field, judging in scale to the players that trotted out onto the field to take their positions. The goal, or orb receptor, was about one half the size of a standard soccer net.

The players were set up in a hockey-type formation with a center, two Tarsi one on each wing, two Tarsi back on defense, and a goalie. An orb was dropped in the center of the field and the two centers ran at it at amazing speed. Dom estimated they were approaching 35 to 40 miles per hour; with complete disregard for safety, they crashed into each other in an attempt to pass the orb to one of their teammates.

Both centers hit the ground after a spectacular crash and both were up in a flash in pursuit of the orb. All players were selfless in their play: willing to give up scoring opportunities and pass if a teammate had a better shot; willing to launch themselves into other players and into the walls surrounding the field if it meant giving their team an advantage. The shots on net were incredible; when the Tarsi kicked the orb toward the goal it was kicked so hard it looked like a rifle shot. The goalie would dive in front of the approaching orb and sometimes it would hit him so hard it would knock him back a couple steps and sometimes down on the ground. But immediately afterward he would spring to his feet and get back in front of the goal. The pace of the game was a pace no human could keep up with; there was checking in the corners, incredible speed, and athletic displays, and Dom thought *This is like hockey and soccer combined on steroids! This isn't a Sox-Yankees game but this will work!*

13.

The next morning Dom went to the café and C'Net and Maria were already there. "C'Net, I watched an orb match last night when I went back to my quarters," Dom said enthusiastically. "The match was incredibly fast-paced and entertaining, the athleticism displayed by the Tarsi was exceptional, and I am very interested in learning more. Maria, you have to see one of these games."

"I am glad you enjoyed the game, Dom," answered C'Net.

Maria smiled and said, "Sure Dom, I will watch a match with you."

Maria had a piece of the red bread, a piece of fruit, and something that looked like a fruit drink in front of her; C'Net had something similar.

"Looks like you guys have the special. I will try the same." Dom's meal appeared in front of him. "Do either of you know how Colonel Jenks is doing?"

C'Net replied, "Colonel Jenks continues to improve. However, he is still sleeping and Doctor Teek informs me he may sleep for quite some time. His body has gone through quite an ordeal, and sleep is the best medicine for him at this time."

C'Net continued, "As requested, I have a transport ready to take us to the observatory whenever you are ready."

Dom and Maria started eating more quickly as if they were racing to finish. Maria spoke first, then Dom. "Ready."

C'Net said, "Let us proceed to the transport in the court-yard," but Dom and Maria were already heading toward where the expected wall opening always appeared.

The transport was an enclosed version of the vehicle they had flown in yesterday. C'Net said "Open" as they approached the craft; the glass enclosure had openings appear in it and they all climbed in. Once inside, the openings closed automatically and C'Net said "Observatory." The craft lifted off and headed for the energy barrier. As they came in contact with the barrier, it seemed to fit an airtight opening around the craft as they passed through and then seal itself. The craft ascended quickly with no apparent G forces and as they passed through each layer of the atmosphere through the upper stratosphere, mesosphere, and into the thermosphere, the light of the day faded into the blackness of space and stars got brighter and brighter until they were brilliant twinkling points of light.

When they cleared the atmosphere what Dom and Maria saw amazed them; construction of the ship to transport the

Tarsi off the Earth was already underway. The asteroid processing facility C'Net had spoken about was anchored to Rahn sub 2 and beams for the superstructure were being loaded onto a type of flatbed transport. There were two transports waiting in line to be loaded; as soon as one was loaded, another took its place. One transport reached its destination and waited patiently for the transport ahead of it to be unloaded. It was as if the Tarsi had a collective consciousness and knew exactly what to do. They worked together in unison as a team with a common purpose. There were so many of them they looked like ants all working together to a common goal: preservation of the nest and survival of the colony.

It was quite an awe-inspiring sight. "C'Net, how could the Tarsi have gotten so much done in so little time?" questioned Dom.

"After we told the system the objective, the system designed the craft that would be optimum for our needs and survival, which could be completed in the available time frame, and with materials that were readily available. We already have the asteroid processing facility; it was a simple matter to move it to Rahn sub 2. Once your message was downloaded and confirmed, Tarsi were sent to Rahn sub 2 to begin the harvesting in anticipation of the design to be completed. Once harvested, the material was loaded into the processor and the system instructed the processor to begin the construction of the superstructure. Detailed instructions are engraved on each structural member, and then put in place and joined with the conveyance. We have to work rapidly; 1.5 orbits will pass quickly when you have a project of this size, and it is a matter of the survival of all Tarsi."

"Oh, that sounds simple; the bureaucrats of our time could learn a thing or two from the Tarsi," Dom said in jest.

"Look how many stars and how clear they are," commented Maria.

"Yes, the star charts you provided show the galaxy has expanded significantly in your time," agreed C'Net. The craft passed by Rahn sub 2 and Dom and Maria stared in astonishment at the manufacturing operation. They continued on to the moon.

"I don't see the observatory anywhere," commented Dom.

"The observatory is on the dark side of the moon; it provides a clearer view of the galaxy, and less interference from the sun."

"We're landing on the dark side?" Dom said in childlike excitement, wringing his hands together. Maria's gaze was glued to the glass in a similar level of excitement.

The vehicle had amazing power and speed. Dom asked, "C'Net, how fast does the vehicle go?"

"The vehicle's cruising velocity in your terms is approximately 217 kilometers per hour or approximately 135,000 miles per hour. We should arrive at the dark side observatory, accounting for deceleration, in just about two hours by your time reckoning."

As the vehicle did a one half orbit around the moon, it began to slow significantly and descend. As they approached the observatory, Maria commented, "You have an energy barrier on the observatory as well?"

C'Net replied, "Yes, the energy barrier on the moon serves a different purpose. It deflects errant meteorites and micrometeorites as well as affords us the luxury of working on the surface without the need for protective suits by maintaining an Earthlike atmosphere and pressure. Coupling this with a gravity field to simulate Earth's gravity makes working on the moon much more convenient."

"Wow, I wonder how Neil Armstrong would feel about this," said Dom. The vehicle passed through the energy barrier just as it had before.

The vehicle lightly touched down in a small courtyard area just outside the observatory entrance and all three got out. The gravity felt exactly as the gravity levels felt on Earth. Dom commented, "I guess no moon bunny-hop for us." C'Net was learning that not all comments required a verbal response; she looked at Dom, nodded, and smiled.

Maria stood outside the vehicle staring at the observatory, somewhat awestruck. It was at least four times larger than any observatory she had ever been in and there were what seemed to be sets of binocular telescopes pointing up at the heavens. "C'Net, that configuration of the telescopes is very interesting; could you explain how they work?"

C'Net explained, "They work on the same principle as the telescopes you used in your own time, but they are significantly more powerful. In addition, the configuration allows us to view most astronomical data collected in three dimensions by linking this moon-based observatory with some of our satellite-based observatories."

"Sounds amazing; I can't wait to see the images," Maria replied. They entered a cavernous room with comfortable reclining seats, their backs facing in toward the center of the room and radiating out from the center in a circular pattern to give the viewers a straight-up view of the ceiling.

"This looks more like a planetarium," commented Dom.

"It is similar. However, the images you see will be in real time and in three dimensions. Shall we be seated?" suggested C'Net. They all sat down and reclined their seats to look directly upward.

"Is there anything in particular you wish to observe first?" inquired C'Net.

"Let's start with this solar system," suggested Maria. A three-dimensional view of the solar system appeared above them and in motion, the planets moving slowly around the sun. "Can I just give verbal commands to the system to change the view?"

"Yes, and you can also view historical data as well. We have archived nearly five hundred thousand years of astronomical data," replied C'Net.

"Zoom out to include the Kuiper Belt and label all planetary bodies in English known in my time," instructed Maria.

The system zoomed out, and all planets and moons of planets were shown with their names next to them in English including the planetoid Sedna in the Kuiper Belt. "Wow. Look at all those undiscovered planetoids in the KB!" Maria exclaimed. "Show the approaching asteroid velocity, distance and size, on a collision course with earth with days until impact," was her next request. An asteroid was highlighted between the orbits of Jupiter and Saturn with the data beside the object: 543 *days to impact, Velocity* 24.9997 *km/ second, distance* 1,173,000,000 *km from Earth and diameter at widest point* 10.035 *km.*

"It's amazing how such a small object so far away could cause so much destruction," Maria said, not expecting a response.

Then Maria asked C'Net, "Have the Tarsi any idea where they may go after they leave Earth?"

"We have for some time been exploring nearby stars for Earthlike planets; one in particular, in fact included in your data, is the star you call mu Arae, which is approximately fifty light years from Earth. In your research you discovered several planets in that system; however, the resolution at your disposal, did not allow you to see all planets in that system. There is an Earthlike planet with water and a cloudy atmosphere that appears to suit our needs, so I will display that planetary system."

The planetary system appeared above them with remarkable clarity, in three dimensions. "How can you get a three-dimensional representation of that system so far away?" asked Maria.

"We observe the system as the planets rotate and revolve around mu Arae, and after we have collected full orbital and rotational data, the system converts the data into a three-dimensional representation. Zoom in on planet four," requested C'Net. The system zoomed in to show oceans, lakes, and plant life. "To date, we have not observed any type of civilization. However, the images we are seeing occurred fifty years ago, so we will not know if that planet is occupied until we go there and explore for ourselves." C'Net explained.

The three of them sat and observed for nearly four hours, yet Maria was still as excited after four hours' viewing as she had been the moment they arrived. C'Net suggested, "Perhaps we should head back to Tarsi City. We have a two-hour flight and Colonel Jenks is up and feeling better. He has requested you join him for dinner."

Dom and Maria looked at each other, and nearly in unison said, "Can we come back again?"

C'Net smiled and replied, "Of course."

14.

The vehicle landed in the courtyard. Maria, Dom, and C'Net headed in to be greeted by Colonel Jenks.

"Colonel Jenks, that rest really agreed with you. You look wonderful," said Maria.

"You look even more healthy that when we first arrived. Did you get some sun today or something?" asked Dom.

Jenks replied, "I don't know what was in that serum but I feel great. No aches or pains, my eyesight has improved, and I can think more clearly than I believe I have in years. In short, I feel as if I could chew nails and spit out rust."

"Why don't we head into the café?" suggested C'Net.

Colonel Jenks ordered steak and salad; the steak was white like chicken but otherwise looked and tasted like corn-fed beef. Dom ordered pizza and the purple drink with less caffeine. Maria ordered assorted vegetables and salad. Colonel Jenks said, "C'Net, it looks as though we may be here for some time and the Tarsi have quite a project on their hands. Is it possible we could get jobs and contribute to the effort of saving the Tarsi?" Dom and Maria nodded in agreement.

C'Net ordered the system, "Please display the top two areas of need Colonel Jenks, Dom, and Maria would be compatible with."

Projected on the wall was:

Colonel Jenks
Transport pilot
Resource harvesting team
Maria D'Luce
Astrometrics
Ship construction
Dominick Costa
System disassembly
Ship construction

C'Net continued, "Displayed are only the top two potential matches; the system will display more if so requested. You are our guests, there is no requirement that you work."

"C'Net, we appreciate your hospitality, but it is not in my nature to be idle, and I will assume not in Dom's or Maria's nature, to sit back and be a spectator. I know I would like to contribute to a project as important as this and could not watch while everyone else is working so hard to save their race. Now from what I see, you could use a transport pilot, that's right up my alley. Let me at those controls."

Dom spoke next. "Ship construction? Go up into space and build a ship that will carry your race to safety? I am in!"

"Astrometrics sounds great, but I think I will work with Dom on ship construction since it's not every day you get to help save an entire civilization," Maria agreed. Dom was delighted.

C'Net answered, "As you wish. All Tarsi will be honored to have the three of you working with us side by side. We do have a request, if you are willing. We would like you to name the ship that will carry us to our new home."

"We would be honored to name the ship. After our meal we will begin discussing options among ourselves, and we will try to agree upon an appropriate name as soon as possible," Maria replied.

"If you all will excuse me, I have some personal matters to attend to. Tomorrow, perhaps we should visit the construction site to get a full understanding of the work you would be doing, and Colonel Jenks could get his first flying lesson on one of our ships at the same time."

"Sounds great," replied Jenks for all three.

"Would meeting here tomorrow morning at oh-seven-hundred by your time standard be acceptable?" asked C'Net. All nodded in agreement and C'Net left.

"Wow, it seems every second here it gets more exciting!" exclaimed Dom.

"Yes, it does," replied Jenks, the smile slipping from his face a bit.

"Colonel Jenks, we really didn't get to know you that well before we left. Did you leave a family behind?" asked Maria.

Jenks replied, "My wife of twenty years, an eighteen-year-old daughter, and a fifteen-year-old son. This will be particularly hard on my son; we were very close."

"I am sorry. I had no idea. But don't give up hope. The Tarsi are very resourceful, so they may come up with a solution to get us back. In fact, I would be surprised if they had not started thinking about it already. Just for fun I will ask the system." She paused. "Do the Tarsi have the capability to return us to sixty-five million years into the future?"

The system responded, *"In principle, this could be accomplished. Professor Seeri is now working on possible solutions to overcome obstacles that would prevent a successful return to sixty-five million years into the future. Projected time for Professor Seeri to complete her work and provide solutions to the obstacles at hand would be six months by your measure of time provided Professor Seeri continues to work at her current rate."*

"I can't believe it, they are already working on sending us home!" exclaimed Dom.

"You see, Colonel? We will be returning home, and you will see your family again, I don't believe the Tarsi will fail; based on what we have seen here, they won't let us down," said Maria.

The smile returned to the colonel's face. "They asked us to name the ship. I think that's the least we could do for them. Either of you have any ideas to start?" Jenks was obviously re-energized by the information.

Dom started, "Well, it's kind of an ark."

"That's good. Maria, any thoughts?"

"How about the Space Ark?" Maria replied.

"That's good I like the Ark thing, where the animals get led in two by two to save them, but I think it needs more. It should be named after someone, the way we name our ships back home," said Jenks.

"That's a great idea, but we are not familiar enough with their history to make a choice like that," said Dom.

"You are correct, but we do know of at least one story where someone saved a race by constructing an Ark, don't we?"

"You mean we should name it Noah's Ark?" asked Maria.

"Not exactly," said Jenks.

"Noah's Space Ark?" Dom threw out.

"How about Space Ark Noah," proposed Jenks. Dom and Maria looked at each other and nodded yes.

15.

The next morning all four met at the café at 0700. "I trust you all rested well?" asked C'Net.

"Yes, and you as well?" asked Maria. C'Net nodded a respectful yes.

Colonel Jenks announced, "We have all discussed your request to name the ship that will take the Tarsi to their new home, and we believe we have an appropriate name for the ship."

C'Net looked pleased and asked, "What did you decide on?"

Dom replied, "Space Ark Noah."

C'Net smiled and asked, "May I know the significance of the name?"

Colonel Jenks replied. "There is an ancient story of a vessel constructed to preserve life on Earth. It was told that rain fell for forty days and forty nights, flooded the earth, and destroyed all life. Noah was considered to be a righteous man; he constructed an Ark, which is a wooden vessel designed to float on water, in which he would carry forth the lineage of man. Noah brought with him his wife, his sons Shem, Ham, and Japheth, and their wives. He also brought specimens of all animals and birds, male and female, in order to repopulate the Earth when the flood waters receded. In order to provide sustenance, he was told to bring and store food. Space Ark Noah will carry forth the lineage of the Tarsi, and this time everyone gets saved."

C'Net looked pleased. "A very fitting name for our Space Ark," she replied. They all finished eating and headed out to the courtyard.

In the courtyard was a much larger vehicle than the one they had taken to the moon the day before. A door swung up and open, and they walked in. "Before we leave, you all should put on the environmental suits we will need today. They are located in the back of the vehicle, and there are rooms in the back of the ship to change into them," instructed C'Net.

"What will we need environmental suits for?" asked Maria.

C'Net replied, "We will be visiting Rahn sub 2 today and the manufacturing facility The energy shield is not on line at the facility as of yet, and there is no atmosphere. You will also need protection from solar flares projected for today. Coronal mass ejections can be fatal to both our species; however, the suits provide complete protection, a full range of motion, and have atmospheric processing. The suit converts the carbon dioxide we exhale back into oxygen and carbon and cleans the air. In case of emergency, the suit can provide breathable atmosphere for up to nine days."

"Quite an improvement on our EV suits," commented Jenks.

After they were all suited and standing in the craft, C'Net asked, "Colonel Jenks, would you like to take the controls?"

Jenks replied, "Sure, but don't I need a learner's permit at least?"

C'Net smiled, and said, "I will explain as we go. The vehicle controls are nearly identical to the vehicle we took to view the city."

The colonel sat behind the controls; C'Net sealed the vehicle for takeoff, and instructed Colonel Jenks, "Pull up on the ball slowly." The ship began to rise. After the ship was at approximately 1,000 feet, C'Net instructed, "Push forward on the ball gently." The ship moved forward, accelerating in speed as the colonel added forward pressure on the ball. The ship passed through the energy barrier, and C'Net instructed, "You may apply more upward and forward pressure on the ball."

The ship rose like a jet fighter, but the gravity inside remained a comfortable one-G. "It's amazing how the ship can accelerate so quickly with no G forces inside," commented Jenks.

"All of our vehicles have gravity-dampening fields that adjust automatically to keep the gravity at a consistent one-G inside," replied C'Net.

Jenks wore a smile of contentment as he took the ship out of the atmosphere and into the blackness of space. "Please head toward Rahn sub 2," C'Net said as she pointed in that direction. As they approached the outline of the superstructure was already taking shape; from what they could see, it looked as if the ship would be about six miles long and three miles wide with several levels.

Dom commented, "It's enormous, but will it be large enough for all Tarsi to live on during an extended voyage?"

C'Net replied, "Unfortunately, a large number of our population will have to travel in stasis. It is planned that several hundred thousand will remain active to tend crops and some livestock that are not traveling in stasis and perform ship's functions. The remainder will sleep; it would be difficult in the time allotted to construct a ship capable of keeping all Tarsi conscious. In addition, by traveling in stasis, we will have to carry much less in terms of food and supplies. The side effect of stasis is that the body ages approximately ten minutes for each year in stasis. If we travel for fifty years the Tarsi in stasis will have aged approximately 8.3 hours—a small price to accomplish a large goal."

Colonel Jenks slowed the vehicle and landed it on Rahn sub 2, about 1,000 feet from the

asteroid processing facility. Hovering loading equipment with powerful lasers were slicing up the small moon and loading chunks into the asteroid processor. Out the other end came the finished components ready for assembly, which were robotically loaded onto the flatbed transport.

Colonel Jenks and the others put on the helmets to their suits and stepped outside.

C'Net walked slowly. Although their boots contained their own gravity field, the gravity of Rahn sub 2 was about $1/12^{th}$

of the Earth's gravity, and if both feet left the surface at once, it would take a bit of time before they came back to get their footing. She went to a panel on the outside of their vehicle and pressed a button; the panel opened and she passed out something that looked like jet packs to each of them.

The jet packs used gravity propulsion similar to the vehicles: they were small, strapped over the shoulder, and had arm rests with a maneuvering ball on each arm. One ball was for direction and one ball was to change orientation. To change orientation relative to work, the wearer would twist the ball clockwise, counterclockwise, or back and forth depending on how he or she wanted to orient him or herself.

"Shall we try our transport packs?" asked C'Net. Without waiting for a response she pushed the ball in the direction of the superstructure, they all followed closely. "Don't worry, there are safety features built into the packs that will automatically avoid collisions with others and objects." They looked like a chain, flying in and out of the superstructure of the ship, connected together.

C'Net explained, "Colonel Jenks, as a transport pilot you would be delivering personnel and materials to Space Ark Noah. This work will begin soon. We must install some of the larger systems within the framework of the superstructure before we tie in all the structural members, otherwise they will be too large to bring inside."

"That can be some tricky flying as the ship gets closer to superstructure completion," stated Jenks.

"Yes, and we are ready to begin now. As you can see, we already nearly have the outside bounds of the ship in place, and before we can install all the supporting structures, we must bring up an energy barrier generator and a fusion reactor. We have a backup reactor and energy barrier generator now being disassembled and loaded for transport, which will be available shortly for you to transport after you complete your training runs," said C'Net.

"Well, you folks don't waste any time. I am good to go as soon as I am needed."

"Yes, bringing a reactor and energy barrier up and getting those systems running are of top priority. Once they are in place and functional, we can enclose the ship and have an atmosphere to work in, which will accelerate the construction process and significantly improve safety."

"You did say fusion reactor?" questioned Dom.

"Yes, the power we need for the energy barrier and gravity drive are considerable. We generate power through the use of element two isotope three, which you call Helium three. It provides plentiful clean power. We had already harvested, processed, and stored all the Helium three from the regolith of Rahn sub 2 prior to your arrival. We have enough fuel reserves to last for thousands of years. In addition to using Helium three for power, it is an essential element in our stasis procedure, which you referred to as cryogenic suspension in your stored data," explained C'Net.

"Amazing, the Tarsi have perfected technology we have only dreamed about," commented Maria.

"What is amazing, Maria, is that human civilization has already conceived of generating power this way, already accomplished space and time travel, in arguably less than ten thousand years of civilization. These same accomplishments took the Tarsi over a hundred thousand years. We are excited to see just how far you will advance over the next millennium. It is possible that humans will be the technological equal of the Tarsi in a very short period of time," replied C'Net.

"I really didn't think of it that way. I guess we have advanced quite rapidly if you put it in those terms. What will Dom and I be doing for work?" asked Maria, changing the subject.

"You two will be on assembly of the structure and the ship itself. You will assist Tarsi in unloading the transport from the asteroid processor and putting the members in place, and then fusing the beams to the structure. Each structural member, what you call an I-beam, will have its location engraved on the side. The receptor on the super-structure will have the same markings, so you will simply match the markings and insert the beam into the receptor. The beam will glow slightly red until inserted properly. Then it will turn to a shade of green until it is fused properly. You then touch the place of joining with the fusion tool and the beam will become one with the structure. Once the beam has been inserted and fused properly, it will glow blue for a short period of time to confirm fusion; then the beam will return to its original color. We then repeat the process until the ship is complete."

"Sounds simple, could we see this procedure up close?" asked Dom.

"Yes, in fact this would be a good opportunity to familiarize yourselves further with the transport packs. Feel free to examine the superstructure and if that's acceptable, we could meet back at the vehicle in two hours," suggested C'Net.

"Sounds great," Colonel Jenks replied first. C'Net headed back toward Rahn sub 2 and the three of them headed into the superstructure. "I have been waiting to get into space for my entire military career; it's hard to believe I am doing an EV walk inspecting a super ship that will save an entire race," said Jenks.

"The most exciting thing I have done in my life was trying to ski down Mt. Killington in Vermont. I ended up walking down. If and when we get back, this is going to be tough to top," said Maria.

Dom had a big grin on his face, twisting the orientation ball and spinning himself like a zero gravity top. "Better slow that down, you don't want to lose it inside your helmet," suggested Colonel Jenks.

The three of them playfully zipped in and out of the beams and construction. Dom and Maria headed up to the top on the structure and stood on the beams using their gravity boots, while Colonel Jenks flew up and inspected the bow. Dom held Maria's hand and looked at her through the helmet glass. "Maria, it's hard to believe a few days ago we were in a lab in Framingham. Now we are in space, on top of the largest spaceship ever constructed, helping to save an advanced race that existed sixty-five million years ago, but the best part of it all is that I am here with you."

"I knew you would get around to telling me eventually," Maria playfully remarked.

The three flew about for the two hours, and then headed back to meet C'Net at the vehicle.

"Did everyone enjoy themselves?" asked C'Net.

"We had a blast. I could have done that all day!" replied Dom.

C'Net smiled through her helmet. "We have nearly an

hour's flight back to Tarsi City, why don't we head back and get briefed on tomorrow's work assignments."

They all loaded their maneuvering packs in the side of the ship, got inside, and headed back to Tarsi City.

16.

Over a year had passed since their first visit to the superstructure. Colonel Jenks had become most proficient at delivering payloads to the Space Ark Noah. The fusion reactor was online and the ship was enclosed inside an atmosphere-filled energy barrier.

The flatbed transports would arrive from what was left of Rahn sub 2, which at this point was nearly completely harvested and wasn't much more than a big rock no more than a mile wide. Transports could pass through the barrier and deliver their payload. The workers enjoyed a zero-G work environment. Once proficient with the maneuvering packs, any worker could unload the transport and move large sections into place for fusing with ease.

The ship was enclosed except for part of a three-foot thick clear dome that covered the top of the ship for cargo delivery from Tarsi City. The dome provided artificial sunlight to grass fields and livestock that already grazed in some sections. The outer skin was nearly complete; Dom and Maria were still finishing the final bow panels. Just above the panel they were installing was written *Space Ark Noah* in both English and in Tarsi.

Through the open panels silver tubes, about two meters long and nearly a meter in diameter, were being loaded to the lower part of the ship that was entirely a Helium-3 refrigerator. It was here that already nearly two million Tarsi were in stasis awaiting their journey to mu Arae. Also, in stasis were some larger cylinders containing ornithomimus, hadrosaurus, and other plants and animals the Tarsi would use to repopulate the new Tarsi Home.

Dom and Maria had become very proficient at the assembly procedure: the component would direct itself to the proper location; Dom and Maria would match the glyphs on the component to the receptor point, insert the beam, and then touch the seam with the fusion tool. The fusion tool was about the size of a claw hammer. Once the seam was touched and the fusion tool activated, the seam would seal itself like a zipper and then disappear. The component would then become a part of the ship with no apparent weld or seam to be found. It was as if the ship was one piece.

Dom and Maria saw Colonel Jenks' vehicle pulling up to the Ark, and decided to pay him a visit. They flew inside the opening in the bow and waited for him to step out. Colonel Jenks' hair had grown considerably and he had a neat beard.

Nearly all the gray had disappeared from his hair, and he actually looked younger.

"Colonel Jenks, you look good. This work agrees with you," commented Maria.

"Good to see you two. You know I love flying, and I always wanted a beard, but the Air Force isn't keen on them. I know this job will end soon, but in some ways I will really miss this. How are you two holding up?" Colonel Jenks asked.

"Couldn't be better. Maria and I are holding our own with the best of the Tarsi construction team, and zipping around like Buck Rogers in zero-G is a great way to spend your day. A little hard on the legs at the end of the day when we land and have to walk on a full gravity surface, but well worth it," replied Dom.

"Where are you staying now?" asked Jenks.

"At our request, the Tarsi have made some temporary quarters for us up here. The hour commute each day back to the city was getting a bit old, and now that we are staying on the Ark, we can get a lot more work done. We only have a little over four months left before impact," replied Maria. "Do you have time to join us for dinner, Colonel?"

"Sure do. I am famished. I've got a full load of Tarsi ice cubes on board that will take a bit for those folks in the environmental suits to unload and stow in that very cold freezer, so let's eat. I've been wanting to try some of Dom's green pizza anyway."

Dom smiled. "Sounds good. You know they can kinda simulate onions and pepperoni," he informed the colonel.

17.

Dom, Maria, and Colonel Jenks entered the onboard café. It was a bit more Spartan than the café they frequented in the City, but had all the same foods available. As they entered the café, Maria noticed C'Net and Keevek sitting at a table together. None of them had seen the two Tarsi in months.

Maria went over to their table. "C'Net, Keevek, it is wonderful to see you both." She noticed they were holding hands. "I am sorry; am I interrupting something?"

"Not at all. It is wonderful to see you all, would you please join us?" asked Keevek quickly. C'Net stood and warmly took Maria's hand, gesturing for the others to come to join them.

"We needed to speak to you all, if you have a moment," stated C'Net.

"Sure," said Dom.

C'Net started, "Shortly after you arrived with your message to save the Tarsi, Professor Seeri and Doctor B'Kla began research into the possibility of returning you to your own time. As you know the asteroid will be here soon, and nearly all the foreseeable problems have been solved regarding your potential return."

"Nearly all?" questioned Jenks.

"Yes. We believe we can safely return you to your own time but there will be a price to pay in the form of aging," Keevek informed them.

"How so?" asked Maria.

"Are you familiar with the Twin Paradox as referred to in your data?" asked Keevek. Dom and Maria nodded yes; Colonel Jenks shook his head no. "If you will indulge me, I will explain the theory to Colonel Jenks." Maria and Dom nodded, and Keevek continued. "Consider twins, one of whom is a space traveler, and the other remaining on Earth. The space traveler embarks on a space journey and the vehicle travels at near the speed of light. When the space-traveling twin returns to Earth, it is discovered that the space-traveling twin is younger than the Earth-bound twin. If each twin had a chronometer, the space-traveling twin's would show less time had passed than that of the twin that remained on Earth. In other words, time passes more quickly on Earth than the time on the spacecraft when the spacecraft travels quickly relative to the Earth. The faster the spacecraft travels the slower time progresses on the spacecraft relative to the stationary Earth."

"How fast can your vehicles travel?" asked Maria.

"We have vehicles designed to travel at high speeds that can reach a maximum velocity of 99.998C or 99.998 percent of the speed of light."

"That's incredibly fast, but even at that speed, it could take hundreds of thousands of years to return to our own time," replied Maria.

"329,750 years, plus or minus," said Keevek.

"How do you plan to return us when the journey will take over 300,000 years?" asked Maria.

"We propose to put you in stasis. However, this is where the problem lies: Tarsi age nearly ten minutes for each year in stasis. If human physiology reacts the same way as Tarsi, you will have aged 6.27 years upon return. For Tarsi, this is a small percentage of our life span, but for humans, this is nearly 7.5 percent of your lifespan. Unfortunately there is insufficient time to experiment and provide a solution for this in the remaining time before the asteroid strike," Keevek explained.

"You are all welcome to join the Tarsi in the voyage to our new home. I hope this has not made you feel unwelcome in any way," said C'Net.

"I am in," said Colonel Jenks quickly. Dom and Maria looked at each other and nodded in agreement. "We are in also," answered Dom for both of them.

"Based on your nature and propensity for risk, we believed there was a 96% chance Colonel Jenks would return and a 91% chance both Dom and Maria would return. We understand your nature and have your return vehicle nearly complete. We also know you all enjoy good surprises," C'Net said with a smile.

"Thank you, I will miss all of you," said Jenks.

"You will not miss all of us. Keevek, Professor Seeri, Doctor B'Kla, and I will be accompanying you," C'Net informed him.

"C'Net, I don't believe you would be entirely comfortable in our time," said Maria.

"I have been selected as an ambassador between our two civilizations. I understand there will be difficulties, but in time they will be overcome. The Tarsi of your time will be there to greet us all as well. Our system will have a contingent of Tarsi there sixty-five million years in the future and I, along with Keevek, Professor Seeri, and Doctor B'Kla, have the honor of not only learning the human culture, but the Tarsi culture of sixty-five million years hence. You could no more talk us out of going than we could talk you out of going. We are all in this together," C'Net explained.

"This should be very interesting," said Dom with a bit of an apprehensive smile.

"There are some other details you should know. First, because of the great amount of time and distance we will not be able to exactly pinpoint the time you left. We believe we can return the ship to within a hundred years of your point of origin in time. Secondly, all of your electronic systems were damaged beyond repair; in fact so damaged the system could not extrapolate the circuitry to replace them. When you arrive in your time, there will be no way to know what year it is unless you travel to the surface and determine that for yourselves. We have a solution to this problem. We propose to send you back slightly before you leave. When you arrive, a team will visit the surface in a small shuttle in a relatively unpopulated area. Then the landing party will determine the local date and time. That date and time will be uploaded to the ship and the departure time you provided to us of your original mission will allow the ship's system to accurately calculate the remaining flight time needed. The ship will automatically retrieve the shuttle, recalculate, and deliver us all to your point and time of departure. To those present, there will have been no time elapsed between when you departed and our return," Keevek explained.

Colonel Jenks, Dom, and Maria were a bit dumbfounded by this announcement; they had no idea that the Tarsi had been working so hard on this problem. "Why don't you all have your meals and then we can visit the ship," suggested C'Net.

None of the humans spoke, they all nodded yes in a somewhat dazed fashion.

Each finished their meals, and C'Net led them to a hanger on the port side of the Ark. Inside the hanger was a sleek cylindrical ship about eighty feet in length with a large retractable door on its side.

"Is that the door for the reconnaissance shuttle?" asked Colonel Jenks.

Keevek replied, "Yes, Colonel Jenks."

There were some markings in Tarsi on the bow. Maria asked, "Is that the name of the ship?"

C'Net replied, "Yes, we felt it appropriate to name the ship in Tarsi."

"What is the name?"

"*Time Messenger*" C'Net replied.

Maria smiled, "That's very appropriate C'Net."

"Could you tell us more about how we will arrive back exactly when we left?" asked Colonel Jenks.

"When we arrive in sixty-five million years, this ship will slow to a velocity of approximately 1.2 kilometers per second in preparation for your mission. The ship has light-absorbing technology and will be extremely difficult to see via land based telescopes. This ship will automatically wake you, Professor Seeri, and Doctor B'Kla from stasis. The three of you will then pilot the shuttle to the surface, determine the date and time, and enter the data into the shuttle's system. Once entered, the shuttle will automatically return and the ship will automatically recalculate time and speed necessary to return to the time and point of departure. You all will then re-enter your stasis chambers and when you awake again, you will have arrived. Colonel Jenks, in the event of a system failure on the shuttle for any reason, you will carry a handheld device to upload the data. Once that is done, you all will be stranded in the time you have landed in, and the device will destroy itself within one minute. If that occurs, you must not interfere with the natural progression of your history," explained Keevek.

"Why send all three of us? I can pilot the shuttle and return to the ship on my own," asked Jenks.

"In the event you fail to return from gathering the required information, the task would fall to Professor Seeri and Doctor B'Kla. They are most familiar with the shuttle and onboard ship systems, so if there are any technical issues, they would be in the best position to correct them," explained Keevek.

"Wow, I have to admit you guys are good. And you always seem to have a backup plan in place," commented Jenks.

Inside the ship were seven chairs, and seven of the stasis

cylinders. They were not much in the way of creature comforts, but then they would be asleep for nearly the entire voyage.

The pilot's chair had the familiar ball control, but there were no windows; it was completely enclosed and the outside was only visible through displays on the walls. There was very little room to move inside the ship; other than the chairs, stasis chambers, and the shuttle, the rest of the ship was all engine and fuel for the reactor that powered the gravity drive.

"Looks like we are riding a bullet home," Dom said to Colonel Jenks.

"I think you're right, but if anyone was going to build a bullet I was going to have to ride, these are the folks I would want to do it," replied Jenks

18.

The months passed quickly, and two days before impact, the asteroid could be seen approaching. It was an ominous sight and was displayed enlarged on a section of the clear dome. Although most Tarsi were in stasis, there were several thousand on the grassy field of the top deck, reserved for recreation and away from the livestock they would use for food on their journey.

All Tarsi technology had been removed from space, and Rahn sub 2 had been completely harvested; it was nothing more than a few floating rocks. The asteroid processor and other Tarsi ships had been stored in hangers aboard the Ark for use upon arrival at the new home world.

All essential items and technology had been removed from

the surface with the exception of the last reactor and energy barrier generator. Colonel Jenks, Dom, and Keevek agreed to return to Tarsi City for the last time and ensure that the reactor and generator were destroyed, and the self-destruct mechanism to do so worked properly. The self-destruct mechanism was insurance that there would be no evidence that the Tarsi ever existed. This was to insure the time line was not contaminated and insurance against a time paradox. It would destroy all buildings, no matter how unlikely the possibility that artifacts could survive and be discovered in the future by humans. Initiating the self-destruct would be the unhappy job of Keevek, Dom, and Colonel Jenks.

"It is a difficult thing to see the only home you have ever known destroyed," commented Keevek to Colonel Jenks on their flight to the City.

"I can't even imagine what you are feeling right now, Keevek, but it was brave of you to volunteer. Someone had to do this," the colonel replied.

Keevek nodded in appreciation of his words.

They passed through the energy barrier and landed in the courtyard outside the building. Dom, Maria, and Colonel Jenks had called home for a time. The city was eerily quiet; nothing moved and there was no sound. "We must first destroy the energy barrier and then the reactor," instructed Keevek.

There were two suitcase-sized containers with handles that Dom and Colonel Jenks unloaded from the vehicle. "What do we do first?" asked Dom.

"First, we must place these devices in a circular pattern around both the reactor and the energy barrier generator," Keevek explained. They all walked to the energy barrier building. Dom and Colonel Jenks each removed four cylindrical objects each and placed them in a circular pattern around the barrier generator. Next they went to the reactor building and repeated the same procedure, then returned to the vehicle. "Let's retreat to a safe distance," suggested Keevek.

The three of them got on board and the vehicle rose to near the top of the energy barrier. Keevek instructed the vehicle, "Thermal devices in place around the reactor and energy barrier generator; initiate devices one through eight." At first nothing happened. Then the building began to glow red, turning to bright red as it slowly crumbled in on itself until all that was left was a pool of glowing red where the building had once stood. The energy barrier immediately dropped, and they were in the open air. "Initiate devices nine through sixteen." The reactor building melted into the ground just as the energy barrier building had, and the city was dead.

Keevek took a deep breath and said "Begin molecular dissociation." The buildings began to change complexion from a smooth marblelike surface to a yellow-white sandy finish. Then they began to crumble like sand castles falling in on themselves. In a brief moment, all that was left of all the Tarsi had built was a small mountain of yellow-white sand.

"Keevek, is that sand?" asked Colonel Jenks.

Keevek replied, "Colonel Jenks, that is partially silica sand and a byproduct of the molecular dissociation which is Iridium. The Iridium should pose no threat to any of the animals in your time."

Dom spoke up. "The K/T boundary is what is left of Tarsi City! Tarsi City will be distributed all over the world; it marks the impact of the asteroid and the demise of most of the world's life forms."

Keevek was visibly moved by the destruction of the city. Colonel Jenks suggested, "Why don't we head home?" Keevek nodded in agreement and the vehicle ascended out of the atmosphere for the last time.

19.

The day had arrived; all the work and preparation was complete. The Ark was a magnificent achievement of hard work and cooperation by all. Grass fields, livestock, and jobs for those who were not in stasis, made it a busy mini-Tarsi City. The Tarsi who were not in stasis would be occupied by tending herds, maintaining the energy barrier, maintaining and feeding the reactor, and cryogenics. Some of the scientists working on important projects remained conscious in the hope that the work would be ready to apply when they reached their new home world.

All that was left to do was watch and wait. All the Tarsi were on the upper deck to watch the spectacular event that was about to unfold.

The system had been moved to the Ark and fully integrated; it displayed the event on the inside of the clear glass dome, showing the asteroid and the Earth closing the gap between itself and Earth. Above the display was a countdown displayed in English and Tarsi: 32 *minutes to impact.*

Dom, Maria, Colonel Jenks, C'Net, and Keevek had met on the upper deck to watch the event together. Professor Seeri and Doctor B'Kla were there also but were involved in discussion amongst themselves about the scientific aspects of the impact.

Colonel Jenks whispered to Dom, "Geeks of any race, they are all the same; their world is coming to an end and they are fascinated by it." Dom just chuckled.

The Ark was already moving to a safe distance and position so the actual event could be seen without watching the display. The asteroid, as seen directly through the glass, didn't seem to be moving that quickly, just a big rock lumbering along.

Maria asked, "C'Net, are you ready for our journey to the future?"

C'Net replied, "Yes, I am looking forward to visiting your time and seeing how the Earth has changed over so many millions of years. It should be quite an interesting challenge to relate to the humans and a more advanced Tarsi culture."

"Are you nervous about the trip?" Maria asked.

"I must admit, I am a bit apprehensive, but more excited than apprehensive. The longest any Tarsi has been in stasis before is three hundred years. In principle, three hundred or three hundred thousand is the same as it relates to cryogenics, but given the extended time period of hundreds of thousands of years, there is a possibility of system failure. There are technicians on the Ark, however, *Time Messenger* is fully automated and however small the possibility is that there will be a problem, the possibility still exists," replied C'Net.

"Thanks, I feel better now," Maria joked.

As the Ark moved further away, the gap between the asteroid and the Earth got smaller and the countdown display read 12 *minutes to impact*.

Dom said, "It's nearly there. I feel like I have a lump in my throat and a pain in the pit of my stomach. For a city like that to be destroyed is a terrible loss."

Colonel Jenks replied, "You're right Dom. This couldn't have happened to a nicer group, but the upside is they are all safe, and if this didn't happen, we could never have existed." Dom nodded in acceptance and agreement.

All gazes had shifted from the system display on the dome and were now looking out of the glass dome at the asteroid itself on its final few minutes before its impact. The Tarsi stood in silence and the display updated 3 *minutes to impact*.

Inside the dome were thousands of Tarsi, but it was dead silent; not one of them uttered a sound as the display counted down silently to 1 *minute to impact*.

The asteroid looked like it was in slow motion as it entered the atmosphere. 5 *seconds to impact* read the display.

Then it happened.

The asteroid impacted directly where Tarsi City had once stood; the amount of energy released was almost unimaginable. It looked as if a large stone had been thrown into a pond as the asteroid pierced the surface of the Earth. The Earth splashed up around the asteroid in what appeared to be a splash of rock and molten rock that covered hundreds of kilometers.

Then the Earth appeared to swallow the entire asteroid.

In an instant a white ring radiated outward from the impact site and traversed the planet.

After the Earth swallowed up the asteroid, as if in reflex, it tried to spit it back out, ejecting material halfway back to the moon in a magnificent eruption.

A dust cloud had begun to radiate outward from the impact site and was beginning to circle the globe.

Some of the ejected material began to rain back down on the helpless planet.

The Earth was burning, and for all intents and purposes it was dead.

It was an event of unimagined power. And if not for losing their city, the Tarsi would have enjoyed witnessing a rare scientific occurrence like this up close.

Unexpectedly, the Tarsi all seemed to be in good spirits, almost jubilant; they were talking, socializing, and nodding in thanks to Dom, Maria, and Colonel Jenks.

Dom was the first to speak. "Why does everyone seem so happy? Tarsi City was destroyed, the Earth is in flames and uninhabitable, and most of your race is in the deep freeze."

C'Net replied "Dom, we are happy because of you, Maria, and Colonel Jenks bringing us the warning. We were unprepared; we did not have technology that could deflect an asteroid of this size, but you can be sure it will be developed by the time we reach our new home. If not for you, we would not be here now. The city would still have been destroyed, but there would be no Tarsi left. Because of you, we have a second chance; we are happy because we live."

"Wow, you folks are really 'the glass is half full' people," stated Dom. C'Net took a moment to think about the reference, then smiled and nodded yes.

"The people of Tarsi would like to give you all thanks once more tomorrow morning, before the Ark begins its journey to mu Arae and you begin the journey to your time. Let us all meet in the café tomorrow at oh-seven-hundred. I will ask Professor Seeri and Doctor B'Kla to join us and we will eat our final meal before we launch, then head to the *Time Messenger*," suggested C'Net.

"Sounds like a good idea. Dom, care to walk me to my quarters and help me pack?" asked Maria. Without another word, Dom and Maria headed off.

20.

At 0700, Dom, Maria, and Colonel Jenks arrived at the café. C'Net, Keevek, Professor Seeri, and Doctor B'Kla were already there.

They stood as Dom, Maria, and Colonel Jenks approached the table. They were all wearing special suits to protect them while in their extended stasis.

All seven of them had on the silver suits, and Dom had to comment, "I feel like a fish ready to be put in the freezer." Maria nudged him as if to stop teasing and Jenks laughed. C'Net continued her coaching of the others on human humor. After C'Net's explanation, the other three Tarsi appeared amused, or as amused as Tarsi could appear.

Although C'Net had expressed some apprehensiveness

the day before to Maria, all the Tarsi seemed in good spirits and ready for the experience.

They all finished their meals. Dom said, "I would like to get some of that purple stuff in a to-go cup. After this long nap, I will probably need some go juice to get myself moving."

C'Net suggested, "Let's head up to the upper deck. All of the Tarsi not in stasis would like to see us off." They all rose and headed to the upper deck. Along the way, any Tarsi they saw made the characteristic nod-bow in reverence, and some even said "Thank you" or "Good luck" in English. It was a humbing experience for the humans to be appreciated so deeply and by so many.

When they reached the upper deck, the system had displayed on the clear glass dome "*Thank you all, best of luck and safe voyage to all of the Time Messenger Team*" with each of the team members' faces.

Dom said, "Wow that's bigger than the display at Fenway. Now I know how Ortiz feels when he hits a walk-off homer."

"Well, Dom, if all goes as planned, you will be able to pick up the season where it left off. You won't even have missed a game, even if you are over six years older. Maybe I could start watching the games with you and you could bring me up to speed on the Sox,"

Maria said affectionately.

Dom hugged her and said, "Of course. I was going to ask you anyway." He paused. "Maria, are you nervous?"

"Of course, you can't see it in these Lost in Space suits, but my knees are knocking. I hope we get this done soon, before I change my mind."

"I know what you mean, being frozen solid for over three

hundred thousand years is a bit unnerving. To tell the truth I am as nervous as you, but I will be right there with you. Besides, look at what the Tarsi have built so far: gravity drive, a space ark, and an energy barrier, to name a few. Everything they have built that we have seen seems to have worked perfectly, so why wouldn't this?"

"Thanks Dom, I feel better," Maria said in a calmer voice.

"Besides, we have a date for tonight's Sox game. I will get an Italian cold-cut sandwich for you from Waverly Market; we'll get some wine and make a night of it," Dom continued.

With that Maria hugged Dom and said, "I am looking forward to it."

"Colonel, you will have a lot to explain to your wife when you get back. Go to work in the morning and come back at night six years older, have you thought that through yet?" asked Maria.

"Honestly Maria, I haven't. All I have been thinking about is just seeing all of them again, and how much I have missed them over the past year and a half. I guess if I had to miss my family for that long, saving a race, this race of people, was worth it. I am anxious to get going, and I hope it will seem like minutes until we wake up and are home. This trip would be classified beyond Top Secret and I will not be able to tell my wife any details. You two will have to understand that if either of you breathed a word, you most likely would be prosecuted and possibly jailed for leaking classified information even if you are civilians. I am sure you will be briefed on this upon our return," Jenks explained, as a father would explain to his child, in a warm and compassionate way, as to warn them and not as a threat.

"I guess I didn't think about that, you're probably correct," Maria replied.

The Tarsi had all gathered on the upper deck, but leaving a path the team could walk through. The elevator would bring them to the hangar where the *Time Messenger* was berthed. As they walked through the crowd, the Tarsi bowed as they passed. As before, some of them spoke in low voices, wishing them "Good luck" and "Safe voyage" in English.

The team reached the elevator. All seven stepped on the platform and looked out at the thousands of Tarsi. Dom waved and yelled out, "Thank you all and goodbye!" The rest of the team waved as well, even C'Net and the others. Thousands of Tarsi waved in return as the elevator lowered them out of sight.

The elevator opened directly into the hangar where the *Time Messenger* was berthed. There were several Tarsi inside and around the ship making final checks.

"All systems on line and ready to launch," one of the Tarsi technicians reported to Keevek.

One of the medical team announced, "*Time Messenger* team, please report inside the ship for stasis preparation." Maria squeezed Dom's arm tighter and they all stepped inside the ship. Once inside, Doctor Teek waited, ready to prepare the team, and began his explanation of the procedure.

"*Time Messenger* team, welcome. As you can see, your stasis pods are open; in a moment you will be entering them for your journey. I will be administering three medications. The first will prepare your system for the stasis medication, the second will be a sedative that will put you to sleep, and the third will be the actual stasis medication that will prevent any cellular damage when your bodies are frozen. After the sedative is administered, you will have ten minutes to enter your pods before it takes effect. After you are all in your pods, the ship will begin its automatic function, closing the pods, initiating stasis, and accelerating into its orbit around the sun. Any questions so far?"

All the team members slowly shook their heads no, looking at each other as if to ask, *Are you all okay with this?*

Doctor Teek continued, "Colonel Jenks, Doctor B'Kla, and Professor Seeri, in this compartment will be stored delivery devices, three for each of you. This will be for when you return from your reconnaissance to determine the current Earth date and time. Upon return to the ship, you will administer the delivery devices in order labeled as one, two, three, and return to your stasis pods. Again you will have ten minutes to return to your pods before the sedative takes effect for your final time destination. Colonel Jenks, the handheld time and date device will be located on the arm of your chair in the shuttle. You must keep this with you at all times in the event for any reason the shuttle system fails and you cannot return to the *Time Messenger.*"

"Understood," replied Jenks.

"Who would like to be first?" questioned Doctor Teek.

Dom piped up quickly, in an attempt to put Maria at ease. "I'll go first." He stepped up to Doctor Teek and extended his arm. Doctor Teek placed the first vial of liquid on Dom's' arm and it drained out into his body, next was the second, and finally the third.

"Please enter your pod," requested Doctor Teek. Dom hopped up into his pod and got himself comfortable.

"Pretty comfy; I feel all warm and tingly," said Dom.

"That is the sedative taking effect," explained Doctor Teek.

"Don't worry Maria, it's a piece of cake," reassured Dom.

Maria bent over and kissed him. "See you tonight," she whispered to him.

"You bet, Sox and subs. See you soon," Dom replied.

After all had received their medication and entered their pods, Doctor Teek and the team once again wished them all well and left the ship.

"Wow, I'm getting pretty woozy," said Colonel Jenks.

"See you all soon," said C'Net.

"Goodnight John-Boy," said Dom. "Sorry, I couldn't resist," he continued. They all nodded off and the pods closed automatically.

After all had drifted off to sleep, their heart rates began to slow and mist began to fill the stasis chamber. Heart rates continued to slow and finally stopped; frost began to appear on the observation windows that exposed each of the faces of the team, and the temperature fell quickly to -250 degrees centigrade, just 23 degrees above absolute zero.

The ship came online, and slowly passed out of the hangar and through the energy barrier as all the Tarsi on the upper deck looked on.

The engines began to hum and a slight vibration came over the ship as the two enormously powerful near-light speed engines powered up. Even if one of the engines failed, the mission could be completed with only one engine.

The ship began its acceleration slowly at first, and then began to increase speed as the distance from Earth increased. As it accelerated more rapidly, Earth became smaller and smaller until it was just another dot in the sky. Not long after, *Time Messenger* was in its final orbit around the sun for its long journey through time.

21.

The ship performed flawlessly throughout the millennia, orbit after orbit around the sun and out of view of any potential viewers from earth.

The ship's chronometer read 329,750 years elapsed mission time, a display beside the mission time read Earth time elapsed 65 million years.

The lights came on inside the ship and then the environmental systems as the ship began to slow. The inside of the ship reached room temperature; three of the pods began warming very slowly, their precious cargo inside slowly began to thaw, and the air inside the pod was purged. It was then filled with fresh air with ionized medication to aid in the process of bringing the three back to consciousness. The pod continued to warm until the three bodies were completely thawed. Then the pod initiated a signal to manually begin their heart pumping and lungs responding to take in the oxygen rich mixture.

Once appropriate body temperatures were reached for Colonel Jenks, Professor Seeri, and Doctor B'Kla, the pod added another ionized medication and stimulated the brain of each until they could function on their own.

Once Colonel Jenks, Professor Seeri, and Doctor B'Kla were able to maintain vital signs without stimulus, the pod doors opened for the first time in hundreds of thousands of years.

Colonel Jenks awoke first. He sat up and saw the pods for Professor Seeri and Doctor B'Kla open, but they were still sleeping. "Professor Seeri and Doctor B'Kla, wake up. Something must have gone wrong," announced Jenks.

Professor Seeri opened her eyes first, then Doctor B'Kla. "Are you awake?" asked Jenks. They both nodded yes. "I just nodded off and woke back up to see you both sleeping with your pods open; we have to check what happened," Colonel Jenks continued.

"Colonel Jenks, your face," Professor Seeri said with some concern. The colonel reached for his face and felt hair. In fact, he had a beard down to his chest, long and black, and hair that reached his shoulders, jet black without a trace of gray.

Colonel Jenks stepped out of his pod gently and his legs nearly buckled under the weight. "I guess I don't have my sea legs yet," he stated. Professor Seeri and Doctor B'Kla did the same but had a bit less trouble standing.

"Professor Seeri, we should check the chronometer," stated Doctor B'Kla. She nodded in agreement. They walked awkwardly to the ship's control panel, looked at each other, and nodded.

"Congratulations Colonel Jenks, you have arrived home," Professor Seeri informed the colonel.

"It actually worked," Jenks said in amazement. "Seems like we only just left, and now we are here!"

Colonel Jenks, Professor Seeri and Doctor B'Kla inspected Dom, Maria, C'Net, and Keevek. "They appear to be resting peacefully, don't they?" asked Colonel Jenks.

"Yes, and look at Dom. He has a beard and hair nearly as long as yours, Maria has very long hair as well," stated Professor Seeri.

"We should refresh ourselves, change our clothing, and prepare to go to the surface." Doctor B'Kla suggested.

"Agreed," replied Colonel Jenks. They showered and changed their clothes. Professor Seeri and Doctor B'Kla changed into typical Tarsi attire: comfortable top and pants. Colonel Jenks came out wearing jeans, a T-shirt, and a flannel shirt over the T-shirt. "With this long hair and beard, I don't think even my mother would recognize me."

"Why did you not remove the excess facial hair and shorten the cranial hair?" asked Professor Seeri.

"We are not sure when or where we will be landing, in the off chance I might run into someone that I know, this is a handy disguise. I can't afford to be recognized, so I felt leaving the hair in place would be for the best right now." Jenks answered.

They all went to the small onboard galley. Colonel Jenks had coffee, Professor Seeri and Doctor B'Kla had a hot drink as well, though none of them seemed to have much of an appetite.

Without much conversation, Colonel Jenks suggested, "If you two are up to it, why don't we head down to the surface and get that intel we need to complete our mission." Both Professor Seeri and Doctor B'Kla nodded. "I will check out the shuttle and have the onboard system run diagnostics. When they are complete and we have the go-ahead, we can leave."

"I will check the handheld time and date device and run diagnostics," Professor Seeri stated.

Colonel Jenks walked into the shuttle bay, and said, "Power up the shuttle." The lights turned on in the bay, the door opened to the shuttle, and the colonel walked inside.

He carried his black luggage bag and stowed it in one of the compartments. He then sat in the pilot's seat and ordered, "Run shipwide diagnostics on the shuttle and report systems status."

All the instruments illuminated and one by one seemed to turn on and off. In a few moments all the instruments were online and functioning.

"*Diagnostics complete, the shuttle systems are fully functional,*" the system replied.

"Prepare the shuttle for launch and our mission to the surface," ordered the colonel.

"*Shuttle preparation underway,*" the system acknowledged.

The shuttle was round with a raised dome on the top and the bottom; the top of the bubble was the crew area, the bottom was where the gravity drive engine was mounted, and the outside ring was where the electronics for the onboard systems and fuel were stored.

Because the upper dome was round, the crew had three

seats, two in the front with flight controls as an emergency backup, and one in the rear for the shuttle pilot, where Colonel Jenks would be seated as pilot.

About twenty minutes later the system announced, "*Shuttle preparation complete and ready for launch.* Time Messenger *velocity is now at launch velocity of* 1.18 *kilometers per second.*"

"System, how has the *Time Messenger* slowed so quickly to 1.18 kilometers per second?" asked Colonel Jenks.

"*The* Time Messenger *deceleration began ten months ago. As the ship approached the sun, the* Time Messenger *gravity field was reversed to push against the sun as we approached, and reversed once again to pull toward the sun as we passed. A more rapid deceleration can be achieved at some risk; however, with the time available this was the safest and most efficient method of slowing,*" explained the system.

"System, what is our current position?"

"*We are now located* 10,000 *kilometers behind the moon, mirroring the moons synchronous orbit around the Earth, using the moon to block any potential sighting of* Time Messenger *from Earth.*"

"I feel like I should say thank you every time I talk to that computer," Jenks muttered under his breath.

"*You are welcome, Colonel Jenks. However, thanks are unnecessary unless giving thanks are a need you feel to verbalize.*"

Jenks thought, *I should have known.*

Professor Seeri and Doctor B'Kla entered the shuttle bay. "We are prepped and ready to launch." Colonel Jenks informed them as he stood in the shuttle doorway. All three took their positions and strapped themselves in. "Begin launch sequence," Colonel Jenks ordered.

The engines started, and the shuttle vibrated slightly in concert with the low-frequency hum of the engines. The shuttle eased itself out of the bay, through the *Time Messenger*'s energy barrier, and into space.

Colonel Jenks pushed on the control ball and the shuttle began to circle around the back side of the moon on its way toward Earth.

22.

As they came around the moon, the Earth was in clear view. Professor Seeri and Doctor B'Kla were glued to the view through the front windshield. "Look at how far the continents are apart!" exclaimed Professor Seeri.

"Look at how the land mass has changed; the inland sea is gone, there are large polar ice caps and there is so much land area," marveled Doctor B'Kla.

"Feels like *déjà vu*. You both sound just like Dom and Maria when we first arrived," commented Colonel Jenks.

The shuttle cleared the moon and headed for Earth, and Jenks thought, *At least things seem to be where they are supposed to be, and we won't have to fight off those velociraptors when we land.*

They were about an hour out and the sun was just starting

to reach the Eastern Seaboard, when the system announced, "*Ship closing in on our position; suggest evasive action.*"

"Can you display the ship?" asked Colonel Jenks. The ship displayed the approaching craft; it was about twice as big as an F-15 fighter, and it appeared to have weapons.

Then it fired some sort of energy weapon that passed in front of them, missing the shuttle by feet. Colonel Jenks pushed hard on the ball and accelerated to the shuttle's maximum velocity, weaving back and forth, utilizing his Air Force training to avoid being hit as he approached Earth.

"That's not one of ours. I have a feeling we have gone too far into the future," Jenks announced as he flew the shuttle in an evasive pattern.

"Professor Seeri, try contacting that ship to see if it is a Tarsi ship from the future firing on us in error" Jenks suggested.

Professor Seeri looked at Jenks as if to say "are you kidding, the Tarsi would never do that," but tried the communication system in an attempt to reach their attackers without success.

Another shot; a narrow miss. Jenks pulled up hard hoping the attacker would fly by, but no luck. He then pushed the ball down hard and they fired again. The energy pulse pierced through the modest energy barrier of the shuttle and hit the gravity drive dome on the bottom of the craft.

"*Warning, gravity drive compromised, system failure in 15.7 minutes,*" the system called out. Jenks pulled the ball hard to the left and got a clear view of the attacker; a beam of light appeared to emanate from space on top of the attacker and within a second it was vaporized.

The shuttle had system alerts going off all over the ship. Colonel Jenks pushed the shuttle to its limit, trying to land before the gravity drive failed. Professor Seeri and Doctor B'Kla had their hands clamped onto the armrests of their chairs as unwilling participants in the attack.

Colonel Jenks got the shuttle into Earth's atmosphere over North America and the system announced, "*System failure in 2.3 minutes*"

Colonel Jenks managed to steer the shuttle to a remote area in the West and about 3,000 feet from the surface the system announced "*System failure in one minute.*"

"Got to get this bird down," said Jenks half to himself. He pushed through the atmosphere and the system announced "*System failure in 10 seconds.*" As he slowed the ship to land the system announced "*System failure in 5 seconds, 4 seconds, 3 seconds …* "

Colonel Jenks managed to nearly land before the system announced

"*System failure.*" They were about fifty feet up; the observation window was facing the surface of the Earth and they began to free-fall.

"*Prepare for impact,*" the system announced. The shuttle fell like a stone and hit the ground hard. Without the shields and gravity control, the front of the ship crumpled, pushing up to the front row of seats and trapping Professor Seeri and Doctor B'Kla.

Without the safety harnesses they all would have been killed on impact.

"Are you two all right?" asked Jenks.

Professor Seeri answered, "Yes, but I am unable to move and Doctor B'Kla appears unconscious. Colonel Jenks, the controls on the ship are damaged; the system has completely failed.

There is nothing you can do for us, but you can save those on the *Time Messenger*. Please take the handheld device, determine the date and time and enter it in. You must leave. I am sure people will be on the way and you can't be seen with us."

"I can't leave you, Professor. I can get you both out," replied Jenks.

"Colonel, it would take hours for you to free us, and we don't even know if Doctor B'Kla can travel if you do. You must not be captured; you must complete your mission or Dom, Maria, C'Net, and Keevek will never return to Earth. You would have a difficult time explaining your presence with us. If we are not in the future and somehow we are in the past, it could affect the timeline and jeopardize the completion of the time displacement equipment in your time. If that happens, all Tarsi will die; you must leave now."

Colonel Jenks nodded in reluctant agreement and said, "I will check on you soon to make sure you are rescued. I will not leave you to die in this ship."

"Thank you, Colonel, but you must leave now before the sun rises and you can be easily seen," urged Professor Seeri.

Colonel Jenks brought them some water, got the handheld time entry device, grabbed his bag and went to the door. He had a bit of a time getting it open, pounding and kicking.

After a few minutes he managed to get the door open enough to squeeze through.

The colonel pushed his bag through the door and placed the time entry device in his pocket. "I will make sure you are all right before I leave the area. We will see each other again soon," he said as he forced himself through the narrow opening.

It appeared they had crashed in an open field; it was dark

and cool. Disoriented from the crash, the colonel began walking just to put some distance between him and the shuttle.

23.

Not long after he began his walk, the colonel came upon a paved road. He thought to himself, *"If I am in the future, at least they still need roads."* He looked in front of him as far as he could see and then behind. There were no other signs of manmade technology other than the road he was walking on.

He walked for quite some time. Then behind him he could hear something approaching, and turned to view the oncoming headlights. It was a very old truck, which looked to be about a 1932 Ford, with sides made out of boards to haul hay and livestock. As the truck pulled up, Jenks tried to make out the license plate, but the glare from the headlights prevented him from getting a clear view, and he didn't want to appear too obvious.

The license plate did not have any reflective qualities, so Jenks got his first indication he was in the past.

The old man driving looked to be in his seventies with nicely cut white hair. He stopped and asked "Need a ride, young feller?" he asked with a southwestern accent.

"Thank you, yes, I am headed into town," replied Jenks.

"You're in luck, that's just where I'm a-headin.' You can toss your bag in the back and hop in; I could use the company," replied the old man. "Long way to town, over seventy miles. You plannin' on walkin' the whole way?"

"No, I was hoping to meet a generous soul like yourself to help me out," Jenks replied.

The old man smiled. "Nice to meet a young feller with manners. Name's Chester, and yours?"

"My name is…Sam," the colonel replied with a bit of hesitation.

"Up mighty early son; need to get to town that bad?" asked Chester.

"No, sir, I woke up early, had a long way to go, and just decided to get started," Jenks replied.

"'Preciate it if you called me Chester; me and sir just don't mix," Chester requested.

"Of course, Chester, be glad to," said Jenks. Chester had a way about him that would put just about anyone at ease; he was disarming and comfortable to talk to.

"Your truck is in great shape. A '32?" asked Jenks.

"Yep, me and this truck are a team, we don't go anywhere without each other."

"I would like to own a truck like this some day."

"Son, you and I are going to git along just grand. Sounds like you're from back East?"

"Yes, I am, from Maryland." Jenks replied.

"Are you from around here, Chester?" asked Jenks.

"Born and raised. Can't see livin' in a city. Like these hills and open spaces where a man can breathe," Chester replied.

Jenks was tempted to ask him the date, but he knew he would get an answer like "the fifteenth," and if he pressed for the year, it might make things uncomfortable. For the rest of the ride, Jenks decided on small talk that wouldn't raise suspicion, letting Chester lead the discussion and hopefully picking up some clues as to where and when he was.

They rolled into town around 5:00 a.m. There was a diner just opening, and Chester said, "Mind if we stop here for a bit son? Nature calls these old bones."

Jenks almost replied instinctively with "Not at all, sir" but caught himself and said instead, "Sure Chester, take all the time you need."

Jenks grabbed his bag and headed in behind Chester. The sign inside read "Please Seat Yourself." Jenks sat at a booth and looked around and thought, *This place is seriously retro; wonder if Jethro and Ellie May are working in back?*

He then turned his attention cautiously to his bag as not to draw any attention. *Well I guess I have arrived back at my projected time on Earth*, he thought, then tore open the corner of the package and peeked inside. On top there was a stack of $10 and $20 bills.

They looked a bit different to what he was used to, older somehow, as he remembered them as a child. Under the bills looked like more letters and newspapers; he pulled out a few bills, stuffed them in his pocket, closed the package back up, and zipped up his bag.

"Be right with ya, honey," the waitress yelled out through an opening behind the counter leading into the kitchen." Jenks just waved as if to say okay.

Chester came out from the restroom and joined Jenks at the table. As he sat, Jenks asked, "Chester, could I buy you some breakfast to thank you for the ride in?"

"Son, that's mighty generous, but you don't have to do that. I was comin' here anyway, and you're good company."

Jenks pressed "Chester, you really helped me out, and it would make me feel better if I could do something in return."

Chester replied, "Son, with you puttin' it that way, I would be much obliged, and thank you."

The waitress came to their table and seemed very excited. Before she asked them what they would like to order she blurted out, "Did ya'll hear about the crash on the ranch south of here, just on the radio? It says the Army is on its way there now."

"When do the newspapers come out?" Jenks asked the waitress.

"Should be here in 'bout an hour or so. What can I git ya?" asked the waitress.

Jenks replied, "I would love some coffee, bacon, and scrambled eggs."

"I'll have the same," Chester chimed in.

"Comin' right up," the waitress replied in a Southern drawl. A few moments later, she brought out the food and placed the plates in front of Jenks and Chester.

"This looks really good," said Jenks, digging in.

"Son, looks like you haven't eaten in a month," Chester commented.

"I just haven't had bacon and eggs for a while," Jenks replied.

"Slow down son, there's plenty more where that came from," Chester warned playfully.

"Chester, I am thinking of getting a car. Do you know of anywhere I might be able to find a decent car for a reasonable price. Mine broke down, and it was in such poor shape, I decided not to put any more money into it. I hate to spend my life's savings, but I have to get a new car, and get back east. " Asked Jenks.

"There is a garage up the street. Friend of mine owns it and has a '33 Olds for sale been tryin' to sell it for a while, askin' $350. Probably take less if you got cash on the barrelhead. You got that kind of money, son?"

"I'll have to count it again, but close," replied Jenks. Jenks knew not to show his surprise at the price; the Tarsi said they were going to send them back before they left, so Jenks had no idea where or when he was.

The waitress brought out the check. Chester stood up and said, "Think I'll visit those facilities again before we leave. If you can hang on a bit, I'll take you up the street to look at that Olds, my friend will be up and he lives in the back."

"Sure, Chester, I will be here waiting." As soon as Chester was out of sight, Jenks reached into his bag and counted out $400 in tens and twenties and stuffed them in his pocket.

He handed a $20 bill and the check to the waitress without looking at it. The waitress looked at the bill and asked "Mister, you got anythin' smaller? We only just opened, and for an eighty-cent check, I don't have enough change in the register yet."

"All I have is a ten, is that ok?" he asked.

"I got eight dollars' change in the register, sorry, mister," the waitress apologized.

"Tell you what, if you can keep this between us, give me back a five-dollar bill and you can keep the rest," said Jenks.

"Yes, sir! Thank you!"

"Remember, it's our secret," Jenks reminded her. She nodded her head yes with an oversized grin.

Chester came out of the bathroom; Jenks stood, and headed toward the door with bag in hand. The waitress paid a farewell visit and on their way out the door yelled, "Y'all come back now."

"Ya made yourself a friend there with that young lady there, son," Chester commented.

"I believe she was talking to you, Chester," Jenks replied.

Chester just chuckled and said, "Let's us have a look at that Olds."

Chester pulled into the Esso service station up the road about a quarter mile, parked the truck and went around the back of the building. After he was out of sight, Jenks put two $20 bills in his glove box.

Not long after, the lights came on and Chester and his friend George came out the front door. George was younger than Chester. He had about five days of beard growth and wore greasy tan overalls with one strap buttoned and a greasy button-down blue shirt underneath. Chester made the introduction, "George, this is a new friend of mine, name of Sam."

George extended a greasy hand to Jenks. Jenks said, "Pleased to meet you," and shook his hand.

George replied with a Southwestern-accented, "Likewise."

Jenks, as career military, knew that because of the accent he was most likely somewhere in the southwest. These two spoke like many people he had run into in his military career, he just couldn't quite pinpoint where.

"Sam here would like to have a look-see at that Olds you're sellin'," Chester started.

"How does it run?" asked Jenks.

"I hate to sell that car. Runs like the day it came off the line but I need the money; not one scratch in the original paint job and I just put in a new clutch," George replied.

George went over to the driver's door, sat inside, put the car in neutral, and turned the key. The car started immediately and idled evenly. Inside the interior looked like new, and the exterior was a shiny black and looked as if it had been lovingly maintained.

Jenks didn't want to get into a conversation with George, so he didn't ask too many questions. "Does it drive as well as that engine runs?" asked Jenks.

"Yes, sir, I will guarantee you that."

"Chester says you're asking $350. Is that correct, George?"

"Yes, sir, it is. If you have cash, I kin let her go for $325."

"You know, George, for a car like that $325 sounds fair if you fill it up with gas and leave on those tags," Jenks replied.

"Don't you want to drive her first?" asked George.

"You just guaranteed me it drove as well as the engine runs and you're a friend of Chester, so that's good enough for me."

"Looks like you have yourself a deal," said George.

Jenks pulled out his wad of cash and counted off $330, handed it to George, and asked, "That's $330, could you write me out a bill of sale please and $5 change?"

"Yes, sir, be right back with it," George replied as he walked back into the station.

Chester looked pleased that he could help. "Nice car, Chester, just like you said, thanks," Jenks said.

"You're welcome son; looks like you put quite a dent in that roll you had. Got enough left to git you where you're goin'?" asked Chester.

"I do, Chester. I have plenty for gas and food to get me back East where my family is from," Jenks replied.

George emerged from the station with a bill of sale in hand, and handed it to Jenks.

Jenks glanced at the bill of sale and saw the date, gulped a bit, trying not to show surprise.

Jenks thanked him as George hopped in the car to pull it up to the pump.

Not long after George announced, "She's all tanked up and ready, sir. I didn't have your name for the bill of sale; you will have to write that in yourself."

"Thank you George, and thank you Chester. I appreciate your help," said Jenks.

"You're welcome, son. I am sorry, but I have to git myself rollin.' I got forty dozen eggs to deliver to the Army base down the road a piece," Chester announced.

Jenks was beginning to put together where he was and now had a bill of sale as to when. He had a good idea which base it was but wasn't quite sure yet.

Jenks went to his car, waved goodbye to both George and Chester, tossed his bag in the back seat, hopped in, and drove off.

24.

The sun was coming up and Jenks was exhausted. He drove back outside town and found what looked like an abandoned building. He pulled around back under an awning, turned the car off, and went to sleep.

Jenks woke up a few hours later. It was hot, very hot. His shirt was soaked with sweat, and he was parched. He got a dry T-shirt from his bag, started the Olds, and headed back to the diner. The diner was busy, most of the stools were taken and all but one booth.

As he walked in, every head in the diner turned to look, some whispered to each other, but they quickly lost interest and turned their attention back to their meals.

The same waitress greeted him cheerfully, "Back again so soon?"

"Yes, ma'am. I would like an ice cold Coca Cola and today's newspaper if I could."

"Comin' right up," she said, as she rushed over to the fountain, poured Jenks a Coke, and grabbed a newspaper on the way back.

Jenks sipped on his Coca Cola and put the paper on the counter. There was no headline about the shuttle crash. He looked up at the date, which was July 1, 1947, and the paper was the *Roswell Daily Record*.

Jenks almost dropped his soda as he did a double take at the paper. He finished the cola and asked the waitress, "What do I owe you?"

She replied, "That's five cents for the cola and five cents for the paper."

"Can you break that five-dollar bill for me yet?" asked Jenks.

"Sure can." She took the bill, took out the dime, and handed Jenks the change.

"That old watch on the counter back there, who does that belong to?" Jenks asked.

"That old thang? That's mine; I set it there cause the buckle comes unhitched and it falls off," she replied.

"How about you sell me that watch?" Jenks asked.

"Sure thang, twenty five cents okay?" she asked.

"That's fine, take out fifty cents and keep the change." Jenks replied.

"Sure!" she replied as she handed him the watch.

"This time right?" Jenks asked, pointing to the face of the watch.

"Yes, sir, keeps pretty good time too," was her enthusiastic response. Jenks nodded and waved on his way out, she once again yelled, "Thank you!"

Jenks was still reeling from the new information, but everything now made sense: the prices, the cars, the décor, and the people. He got in the Olds and headed east, looking for somewhere he could inspect his mysterious package uninterrupted. He also had a job to do by uploading the date and time to the *Time Messenger*.

He drove for several miles, and found a dirt road leading off the main road; he followed the dirt road until he was far enough that he couldn't be seen. Jenks pulled over and pulled out the package. On top it seemed as if there was about $10,000 in $10s and $20s, all vintage bills older than 1947.

Under the bills there were sections of newspapers and two other packages, one marked for President Harry S Truman, *President's Eyes Only* and another package for *Professor Einstein*.

Also enclosed was another letter to *Colonel Jenks* with the seal of the President of the United States.

Colonel Jenks opened the letter and read:

Colonel Jenks:

Congratulations on your return to the 20th century. Your mission is to head to Princeton University in New Jersey and secure the cooperation of Professor Einstein in the development of the gravity well for the time displacement equipment. Professor Einstein's address is 112 Mercer Street at Princeton.

This co-operation will be most easily accomplished by deliver-

ing to him the enclosed package; the material inside will ensure his cooperation. Once this is completed, Professor Einstein is to set up a meeting with President Truman at the White House and have him invite my father to attend. My father is currently a student at Yale, living off campus in New Haven. There is a letter enclosed for my father as well.

There can be only four humans other than yourself who understand the full implications of this project: President Truman, Professor Einstein, and my father, who will in time explain the situation to me. We must ensure that the mission is completed and the Tarsi survive. The Tarsi are our allies in 2007 against an intergalactic threat, which threatens the entire human race. If they do not survive, we as a race will not survive.

This will be a long and lonely mission. I am sorry I cannot be there to help you.

Good luck, Colonel. The world is depending on your success.

Signed

President George W. Bush

"Nothing like a little pressure to start off your day. Just meet with Professor Einstein, the president, and a future president, and develop technology to save the world. Piece of cake," Jenks muttered.

Jenks took out the handheld time entry device, entered July 1, 1947, then looked at the waitress's watch and entered 8:35 a.m.; the device requested *"Please enter time zone or location"* Jenks entered "Roswell New Mexico" and thought, *These guys think of everything.* The device announced *"Time, date, and location upload to Time Messenger successful. Please place the time entry device on the ground and step away; self-destruct in one minute."*

Jenks walked about fifteen feet away from the Olds, put the device down on the ground, and it began to turn into a yellow-white just as the Tarsi City buildings had done. In exactly one minute all that was left was powder.

Jenks thought, *I hope they all have a nice sixty-year nap; likely I won't be here to greet them, but time to get to work. It's off to Jersey.*

Jenks hopped in the Olds and headed east to meet one of the most prominent scientists of all time.

25.

It was before 9:00 a.m. on July 1st and it was already hot. Jenks headed east and drove day and night, stopping only for food, fuel, and maps. As he was driving he thought, *President Eisenhower was correct; we definitely need an interstate highway system.*

Jenks arrived at Princeton about 2:00 on July 3rd, and after some directions arrived at Professor Einstein's home about 2:30. Jenks parked the Olds, got out, and stretched; he had been driving nearly fifty-four hours straight through, stopping only for catnaps and coffee. Jenks thought, *What kind of impression will I make looking like this?*

He got the package from his bag for Professor Einstein, and knocked on the door. A few moments later a woman answered and asked, "May I help you?"

Jenks replied, "I would like to see Professor Einstein, if I could, please?"

The woman replied curtly, "Professor Einstein is working and cannot be disturbed." Colonel Jenks offered her the package. There was a letter attached to the top of the package addressed *For Professor Einstein's Eyes Only, Top Secret, Top Priority*. It had the seal of the President of the United States. She took the package, looked a bit concerned and said "Wait here," as she closed the door.

A few moments later, Professor Einstein was at the door. He spoke to Jenks with a German accent. "Come in please, Colonel, we have much to discuss."

Jenks followed Professor Einstein into his study; there were blackboards with equations, books and papers everywhere. Professor Einstein moved some books from a chair near his desk and offered Colonel Jenks a seat.

"Colonel, what is in this letter is fantastic, from a president sixty years in the future, and is very hard to believe. It claims you have been back in time and returned to 1947 in a spacecraft that crashed in New Mexico. It also clams that you returned based on my work on special relativity," stated Einstein.

"Yes, sir. I am not a physicist, but I traveled with two physicists; they are still in orbit around the sun and will return in 2007. We could not predict our exact time relative to the year 2007, so I and two Tarsi scientists from sixty-five million years ago returned to determine a time reference that could be programmed into our ship for the others to return. We had planned to return to the mother ship and arrive in 2007, but our shuttle crashed in Roswell, New Mexico and they have been captured by the military," Jenks responded.

"I see, but as you can imagine, this is quite hard to believe."

"Sir, I understand. If I were in your position I would find it hard to believe also, but I see that some math equations have been provided to you. What are those?" questioned Jenks.

"That is what got you in the door, Colonel. They are an extension of the work on gravity I did in 1912. This is fantastic. If these equations are correct, I could not have accomplished this in a lifetime's work," Einstein replied.

"I assure you they will work. My mission is to secure your help in the development of the gravity well for the time displacement equipment. If you refuse, all humans on the face of the Earth are doomed," Jenks warned.

"I see. Colonel, what is this device?"

Colonel Jenks walked over to the professor's desk. "That is a laptop computer, Professor."

"A computer? How is it possible a computer could be contained in such a small package? ENIAC is the most sophisticated computer on the planet and it takes up an entire room. Can you demonstrate how such a device works?" questioned Einstein.

Jenks opened the laptop and pressed the power button; the welcome screen lit up and the message *Welcome Professor Einstein* appeared. It was a specially designed laptop and keyboard for solving complex math functions.

"I am not a computer historian, but I believe you will find that this is many thousands of time more powerful than any computer available today," Jenks informed the professor.

Jenks tapped the Enter key and said, "Professor, why don't

you try entering an equation you already know the solution to, to test the computer?"

"Sounds like a good idea." Einstein replied as he entered a complex calculus equation, and asked the colonel, "What is next?"

The colonel replied, "This system is a bit more advanced than I am used to, but there is a 'Solve' button. Let's give that a try."

Professor Einstein pressed the Solve button and the computer responded, "Enter the summation upper limit." Einstein entered a number. "Enter the summation lower limit." He entered theta, and the computer continued until all the integration limits, angles, and trigonometric functions were entered. The computer responded, "Entry complete, press solve."

Einstein pressed the Solve button, and the answer displayed on the screen. "Oh my goodness!" Einstein exclaimed.

"Is that correct, Professor?"

Einstein pointed at the enormous blackboard with nearly every square inch covered in equations. There, circled on the bottom right-hand corner, was the same answer. "That took me a week to solve! This is an incredible gift."

"This will run on battery power for several hours, but you must plug it in to recharge it.

It says on the recharger there is a built in surge protector, to protect your system from power available in 1947. Also it appears there is a manual to explain all the functions," Jenks informed the professor.

"Professor, no one must ever see this computer but us and the people we bring into our team. We would have a difficult time explaining this technology to anyone of this time," warned Jenks.

"I understand. Colonel, may I inquire as to when you will be born?" Einstein replied.

"I will be born in 1962; this is a bit odd for me. I am here in 1947 and won't be born for another 15 years," Jenks replied, showing Einstein his driver's license.

"Yes, it would be most important to avoid your family during this time. You must not interfere with your decision to join the military, that could have dire consequences," Einstein warned while examining the driver's license.

"I understand. Professor, did you see this in your package?" asked Jenks.

"The newspaper?" Einstein questioned.

"Yes, sir; this is tomorrow's paper if you need further convincing."

Einstein picked up the newspaper and examined it closely. "Tomorrow morning will confirm your story. However, for now I am sufficiently convinced that this computer and the mathematics you provided are not available in 1947. But what is next? How do I help?"

"We need to meet with President Truman, warn him of this threat, and enlist his help and the help of a future president, George Bush, currently a Yale student living in New Haven. Can you get us in to see him?"

"Let me try," Einstein replied, still a bit shaken by the events that had just unfolded. Einstein picked up the telephone, and an operator answered. "Please get me the White House."

The phone rang once and the answer was "White House."

"This is Professor Einstein calling from Princeton; could I please speak to the president?"

The voice replied, "The president is in a meeting at the moment, could I relay a message?"

"Yes, please tell the president that Professor Einstein is calling on a matter of utmost urgency and a matter of the security of the nation," Einstein replied. The voice replied, "Yes, sir, I will deliver the message to him."

Einstein hung up the phone, and Jenks looked worried. "You didn't expect the president to just pick up the phone, did you? They are just checking to make sure it was really me that called," Einstein explained to put the colonel at ease.

A moment later the phone rang; Einstein answered. "Hello," the voice on the phone said. "Please hold for the president."

"Professor Einstein, this is an unexpected pleasure; how are you?" President Truman asked.

"Very well, thank you. We have a situation that must be addressed immediately and in person, could we come to meet with you please?" Einstein asked.

"Of course. I'll have a car on the way to pick you up for an 8:oo a.m. meeting," replied President Truman.

"I will be bringing someone with me, and could you please have someone pick up a George Bush and have him brought to the meeting as well? He is a student at Yale, living in New Haven."

"Is that Prescott Bush's son?" asked President Truman.

"I don't know, but he is essential to the meeting; it would be best if he didn't have too much time to inform any of his family as to where he is going, since the information we will be discussing will be quite sensitive."

"I will have him here when you arrive. See you soon," ended President Truman.

"Well, I guess you have a bit of clout, Professor," Jenks commented.

"In some cases, in matters of national security, where I have been involved with the government before, they will at least listen to me. Do you think you will have any trouble convincing President Truman? He may not be as receptive as I was," replied Einstein.

"I don't believe that will be much of a problem. I have a package and a letter for him as well, and with you adding to my credibility, I am sure we can bring him on board to save the world," replied Jenks.

"Would you like to prepare yourself for the meeting with the president?" Einstein continued.

"Yes, I would, thank you. I will get my bag from the car and be right back."

Jenks went out to the Olds, retrieved his bag, and for the first time took a moment to look at the newspapers that were enclosed. "Well this should help!" Jenks exclaimed.

He went back inside, and showed them to Professor Einstein, "Professor Einstein, I don't think securing financing for this will be a problem. It looks like I have sections of the *Wall Street Journal* stock prices, one section for each year, for the next sixty years," Jenks informed Einstein.

"I believe you are correct. What is in that small bag?" questioned Einstein. Jenks emptied out the bag on the table and what poured out were perfectly cut diamonds.

"I guess we will have the money we need to get started,"

Jenks said, a bit stunned. "I guess nothing should surprise us from here on out."

Einstein had his housekeeper prepare food and a guest room for Jenks while he showered.

"Professor, would you mind if I got a little sleep? I have been up for over two days driving here from Roswell."

"I will have my housekeeper prepare a room for you, but first, eat something. There is food on the table and we should both get some rest. The car will be here very early in the morning," Einstein informed Jenks.

"You're a lifesaver," Jenks thanked Einstein.

"Let's hope you are correct," Einstein joked with Jenks.

It was exactly 4:00 a.m. and there was a military officer knocking at the door with a car to take them to the White House.

"Professor Einstein, I am Sergeant Pierson; I will be your driver to the White House."

"Good morning, Sergeant. Wonderful morning for a ride, isn't it?" Einstein responded.

Jenks and Einstein both grabbed their bags and got in the car. "Sleep well?" Einstein asked Jenks.

"Like a baby. Funny how going without sleep for over two days will tire you out," Jenks replied.

"Yes," Einstein chuckled.

26.

They arrived at the White House just before 8:00 a.m. Sergeant Pierson stopped at the entrance; the guard looked in the car and waved them through as if expected.

Once inside, two men in black suits greeted them, quickly asked for their bags, and quickly went through them. Then one stated, "Gentlemen, please follow me."

They were led to the Oval Office where President Truman was waiting along with a very bewildered-looking young George Bush. "Professor Einstein, wonderful to see you again, and who is your guest?"

"This is Colonel Jenks with some remarkable information," replied Einstein.

"Do you all know each other?" President Truman asked.

"I only know Mr. Bush by reputation, but he is essential to what will be discussed here," Colonel Jenks replied. Einstein nodded acknowledgement in George Bush's direction.

"Well then, I am anxious to hear this remarkable information," President Truman replied.

"Mr. President, what I have to tell you is quite sensitive, and for our ears only," Jenks said as he gestured toward the two men in black suits who were waiting near the door.

"Jim and Ron, would you please excuse us? We have some sensitive information to discuss."

"Yes, sir," they replied in unison, and then stepped outside the Oval Office and closed the door behind them.

"Now what is so sensitive, Professor?" requested President Truman.

"Sir if I may, I have something for you," Jenks interrupted. The two men had opened Jenks' package for the president and the envelope to verify there were no weapons, but did not look at the content. Jenks handed the letter to the President. It had a presidential seal and was simply addressed *President Truman*. Then he handed another to George Bush, also with a presidential seal.

While President Truman read the letter, Jenks looked at the previously wrapped newspapers; the letter read:

Dear President Truman

The actions we take here today will affect all of mankind; in fact, they will affect the survival of the human race. What I tell you will seem too fantastic to believe, but I assure you all of it is quite true, so please keep an open mind as you read this letter.

The colonel sitting in front of you is a time traveler. He returned to your time in a ship that crashed in Roswell, on July

1, 1947, *with two scientists from another race who are now being held at the Army base in Roswell. The two scientists' names are Professor Seeri and Doctor B'Kla. They will not speak to anyone until they speak to Colonel Jenks. If you call Colonel William Blanchard, commander of the Roswell base, he will confirm what has crashed and the two guests inside.*

These two scientists are our honored guests, and should be treated as such. The craft should be taken and stored in a hangar at Wright Field in Dayton, OH, and the guests made as comfortable as possible in the complex below the hangar.

Enclosed are The Roswell Daily Record newspapers from July 2nd through July 8th for you to easily confirm this letter and also to show you the course of action to take over the next few days.

The Colonel has gone back in time and brought information to the Tarsi race that existed on Earth prior to human race. The information that he carried allowed them to save their entire race. In time the Tarsi will save the human race from a race of aliens called the Grays that have designs on our planet. It is imperative that the Colonel completes his mission to make sure that the time displacement equipment gets built for the trip back in 2007. He will need the help of Professor Einstein and the two Tarsi scientists in custody.

The Tarsi and humans need each other for each of our races to survive. If the time machine does not get built and we do not go back in time to save the Tarsi, the Tarsi will not exist to save the humans.

No one other than the people in this room and myself must know the full implications of this project; if for some reason the time displacement is not completed on schedule in 2007, both races will perish.

By the way, I am quite an admirer of your presidency, sir. You have already had to make hard choices to end the war, and now you have to save the entire planet. History will show that there is no better man for the job, and in a very real sense, you have already succeeded.

Best of luck, and God bless.

Signed

George W. Bush

43rd President of the United States

President Truman dropped back in his chair with his mouth hanging open a bit in astonishment. President Truman then turned his attention to George Bush.

"Mr. Bush, this letter is signed George W. Bush. do you know anything about this?" asked President Truman.

George Bush had just finished reading page one of his letter letter, the bottom of page one of his letter read

Dad,

You may discuss the contents of page one of this letter with those present. Please do not let anyone see page two of this letter, quickly put your letter back in the envelope and in your pocket. Read page two when you are in private, then destroy the letter. Do not let anyone know about the contents of this letter, not even Mom, it must be our secret.

With love, your son,

George

George Bush quickly put his letter back in the envelope and tucked the letter in his pocket while President Truman was consumed with reading his own letter.

"Mr. President, I have just read my letter, also signed George W. Bush. I am George H.W. Bush. My son is

George W. Bush, and he is currently one year old. These letters are from my son in the year 2007; he tells me I will be vice president to Ronald Reagan for two terms, and then I will be the forty-first president. I will be responsible for recruiting Colonel Jenks to the project in 1992 and bringing him in when the time is right. I am as confused by this as you are," replied George Bush.

President Truman pressed a button on his intercom and said, "Marge, would you please get me Colonel William Blanchard at the Roswell base in New Mexico."

A few moments later the intercom buzzed and said "Colonel Blanchard is on the line, sir."

"Thank you, Marge," President Truman responded, and picked up the telephone. "Colonel Blanchard, good morning."

"Good morning," the colonel replied.

"I understand that we have recovered a vehicle and two travelers, is that correct?" asked President Truman.

"Yes, sir," the colonel replied.

"Have they spoken to you?"

"Not a sound, sir."

"Please bring a telephone to them; I have someone here they will speak to," President Truman ordered. "We'll wait on the line."

"Yes sir." In Roswell, Colonel Blanchard made his way to the building where Professor Seeri and Doctor B'Kla were being held, brought in a telephone, held it up to his ear to demonstrate how to use it, and handed the telephone to Professor Seeri. "Go ahead, sir," Colonel Blanchard spoke into an extension as he waited for a response.

"Hello, this is Colonel Jenks."

"I am so glad to hear from you Colonel, this has been a trying situation," responded Professor Seeri.

"We are going to get you to more comfortable accommodations, Professor, and I will meet you there. It is acceptable to communicate your needs to the people there, but nothing about the mission; there is more you need to know. I will meet you soon," Jenks informed her.

"Colonel Blanchard, these people are to be treated like VIPs. Give them whatever they need. Colonel Jenks, George Bush, and Professor Einstein will meet you at Wright Field shortly. Prepare them and the ship to be moved to Wright Field. Get going on a press release that we recovered a downed weather balloon," Truman ordered.

"Yes, sir," Blanchard replied.

"It is going to take me a few moments to digest this," Truman said after he hung up. "We are under attack by an alien race we have never seen, there are time travelers here to make a new time travel machine that won't be ready until 2007, I have met one future president, and have a letter from another who is his son, and it isn't even 9:00 a.m. yet. This should be quite a day!"

"Yes. Mr. President, may I show you a gift I received to work on this project? This is a computer that won't be available for another sixty years." Einstein demonstrated his laptop to the president, who still had an astonished expression on his face.

"Marge, please make arrangements for the four of us to travel to Wright Field," President Truman spoke into the intercom.

"Yes, sir," was the reply.

"Me too?" questioned George Bush.

"You are now an important element in the development of the machine that will save billions of people. I will have word sent to your wife; you will be back soon," President Truman informed him.

Epilogue

Over the years Einstein, Colonel Jenks, and the Tarsi scientists became close friends. Professor Einstein and Colonel Jenks became especially close, taking many afternoons sailing on Lake Carnegie while discussing the time displacement project. On April 18th 1955, Albert Einstein died of heart failure and Colonel Jenks decided it was time to disappear to the outside world as well. Colonel Jenks changed his name and moved away, so not to be tempted to look in on his family as time wore on.

In the year 2007, Time Messenger arrived on schedule. RV1 had disappeared only ten minutes when the team reappeared over the Area 51 complex. Time Messenger landed and Dom, Maria, C'Net, and Keevek stepped out of the craft. Maria had hair past her waist and Dom had hair to his shoulders and a long beard.

As they stepped out of the craft, they saw another spacecraft crashed on the ground with two small gray aliens being taken into custody.

Mr. Ross came to greet them. "Welcome back. I trust you had an interesting trip."

Dom spoke up first. "You weren't kidding when you said this is a trip none of us would ever forget. Who are those guys?"

"Dom, those are Grays, aliens who are our enemies. I will brief you all on this in just a few moments. They fired an energy beam at the main generator while you were in the time displacement machine and caused a power surge, which sent you back sixty-five million years," Ross replied.

"How did you know…" started Dom.

"Soon I will explain all," promised Mr. Ross.

"Where are Colonel Jenks, Professor Seeri and Doctor B'Kla?" asked C'Net.

"Professor Seeri, Doctor B'Kla and Colonel Jenks crashed their shuttle in 1947. Professor Seeri, Doctor B'Kla are here, but Colonel Jenks would be 105 years old," Mr. Ross responded.

"Colonel Jenks' family… is there anything we can do?" asked Maria.

Dom, Maria, C'Net, and Keevek look visibly upset by this new information.

"Don't worry, Maria. I will see to it they are well taken care of," Mr. Ross replied.

"Dude, look at your hair and beard, and Maria how did

your hair get so long. Look at those little guys. I knew there had to be aliens!" Mark said with the excitement of a child.

"Come, it's time to debrief you, follow me," Mr. Ross said as he started walking to an open area about 100 yards away from the building.

As they walked away from the complex into the open area, a spacecraft decloaked, and a ramp extended to receive them. Mr. Ross continued walking directly into the ship; the others followed somewhat apprehensively.

Once inside the ship they all entered a conference room where there were two beings seated that looked somewhat like Tarsi, but smaller in stature, President George W. Bush and his father, former President George H.W. Bush.

"Please sit down," invited President Bush. "This is Zita and Vico of the Tarsi home world." Zita and Vico nodded in the familiar Tarsi bow.

All looked stunned, including C'Net and Keevek.

President Bush started the debriefing. "I have quite a lot to tell you, first of all, the Tarsi are all alive and well and have settled in nicely on the new Tarsi home world in the mu Arae system. We are the best of friends. We have worked together all these years since the return of the shuttle in 1947. Professor Einstein, Professor Seeri, and Doctor B'Kla worked tirelessly to make sure the time displacement equipment would be completed on schedule.

"There is a race of very aggressive aliens we call the Grays," he continued, "who wanted to lay claim to Earth several million years after the meteor strike sixty-five million years ago when the Earth was relatively uninhabited with life. The Tarsi tried to explain to them that the world was spoken for but they were quite insistent, to say the least. The Tarsi have cloaked bases on the dark side of the moon and cloaked underwater bases here on Earth to protect us. Otherwise the human race would never have had a chance here on Earth. If that had happened, we would not have developed the time displacement system to go back to save the Tarsi. The Tarsi have been defending Earth for millions of years waiting for our arrival.

"We could not reveal the existence of the Tarsi for fear it might have interfered with the timeline and development of the time displacement equipment. If that happened, of course, all of us would just have ceased to exist." He paused. "Now that you have gone and returned safely, there is no need to keep our friends the Tarsi a secret. It was the Grays that shot down the shuttle, and their craft was destroyed shortly after they opened fire on you. We believe they got wind of what was going on here and tried to take out the generator before you went back. The good news is that the Tarsi will be installing a planet-wide energy barrier now that we can reveal their presence, and this should finally discourage the Grays for good."

"But how could you have known so much in advance?" Mark asked.

"I can answer that for you, but I have to take care of something first," Mr. Ross responded.

Mr. Ross picked up a small bag on the floor and headed out of the conference room; about ten minutes later he returned, with a short black crew cut and clean-shaven, but in Mr. Ross's baggy clothes.

"Colonel Jenks!" Maria exclaimed.

"Yes, I was sick and tired of bleaching out that hair and beard. I had to wear a hat all the time because the black roots would grow in so quickly. I had to disappear until the trip back was successful. Mark, as you have figured out by now, I knew so much because I was there. Fortunately, since I was there, I didn't see the harm in sending back some of our food compositions for us. I couldn't do that to Dom and Maria or my younger self again. Grass and ornithomimus gets old quick," Jenks explained.

"How is this possible? You should be over a hundred years old, but you look…" said Maria.

"That Tarsi serum. I got progressively younger until I reached about twenty-five years old by my estimation and have aged slowly since then. I really don't know how I will age or how long I will live. Since I took the serum, I have not been sick a day. It is remarkable how energetic and young I feel at 105 years old. It's amazing how some hair, baggy clothes, glasses, and a little makeup can completely change the way you look," Colonel Jenks replied.

"Incredible; I would never have put that together," Mark commented.

"I have something for you." Jenks reached into his bag, took out three small books, and handed them to Dom, Maria, and Mark.

"What's this?" Dom asked as he opened the book.

"That's twenty-five million for each of you to get started. Saving the world has its perks. And here's something special for Dom and Keevek," Colonel Jenks said as he handed Dom and Keevek each a small box. Dom and Keevek opened their boxes; each contained a diamond ring, made from diamonds that were sent back with Colonel Jenks.

"It is our custom to give a lady a diamond ring when you

plan to spend the rest of your lives with them," Colonel Jenks explained to Keevek. "Don't worry, ladies, they would have gotten around to it eventually on their own."

The two couples smiled at each other and held hands. Everyone sat there stunned with the new information they had just received.

"Colonel Jenks, are you anxious to see your family? And why the name Ross?" Maria asked.

"It's been sixty years and I have a lot of explaining to do, but I can't wait to see them all again. As far as the name goes, Professor Einstein used to jokingly call me Mr. Roswell in private because of the crash. I just shortened it to Ross," Jenks replied.

"I have some more good news. Now that we can reveal the Tarsi, we can make a serum, slightly modified from the serum Colonel Jenks received, that we believe will cure all human disease. I can speak from personal experience. I was given a very small dose of the serum when I had skin cancer. I have been mentioned as the most-fit president in history by Matt Drudge since then. Also, the Tarsi have perfected travel through artificial wormholes, so we can travel to anywhere in the universe instantaneously. You all can visit mu Arae whenever you want. Colonel Jenks, I would like you to be the ambassador to the Tarsi home world after you have time to become reacquainted with your family.

Also I guess we owe you sixty years back pay. Mark, Maria, and Dom, I have some new adventures in store for you as well," President Bush announced.

"As it turns out, I don't think I will need that back pay. I hope my wife and kids will like their new mansion, even though they will have to give up the apartment and small yard. The rest sounds good. I just wish my friend Professor Einstein were here to see how this all turned out," Jenks replied.

"I have some good news on that front as well," President Bush replied, as a man in his late thirties walked in the room.

"Professor?" Jenks questioned in bewilderment.

"Yes, Colonel; it is good to see you again as well," Einstein replied.

"How is this possible?" Jenks asked.

"On April 17, 1955, I had a mild heart attack no one knew about. The Tarsi replaced my body with a duplicated body that simulated a fatal heart attack on April 18th. I was given the same serum you were given and my body completely regenerated itself; not bad for 128 years old. Since April of 1955 I have been living on the Tarsi home world. We could not reveal this to you for obvious reasons," Einstein replied.

As Jenks gave Einstein a warm hug he said, "We have some sailing to do as soon as I get back."

"I would not miss it for the world," Einstein replied.